"Witt, it was amazing. And under any other circumstances..."

Marina let her words trail off. Her world, her job, didn't allow for more than they'd already had. And she'd seen firsthand the heartache her parents had gone through when they'd tried to mix love and danger. No thanks.

Witt's ice-blue eyes revealed nothing, but his palm wrapped around her jaw and he pulled her face to his for a last, searing kiss. "This isn't over," he said and let her go.

Her heartbeat went into triple-time. But he made no further comment.

She took a breath and forged through the door. His light footfalls followed her out into the blinding Paris sun.

A muffled *pop* echoed off the quiet wall of the neighborhood. They both froze. Next to Marina's foot, a cobblestone exploded.

Another *pop* sounded. And Witt growled a curse.

Bloody hell, someone was shooting at them!

Dear Reader,

Welcome back to the continuing adventures in the MISSION: IMPASSIONED miniseries! My hero Dewitt von Kreus's South African background is the product of my longtime interest in the continent, and it enabled me to touch on a complex political situation of which most are unaware. Next time you buy a diamond, ask where it came from. Ask for proof.

Naturally, such a classic tortured hero deserved the strongest heroine. Where better to find her than the hallowed halls of the British Secret Intelligence Service? Marina is like none other. Sexy? Sure. Sassy? Absolutely. She definitely knows how to take care of herself…and her man, too.

Working with the authors of this series has been an utter delight. A more talented, more professional group of ladies can't be found. If you enjoyed this Silhouette Romantic Suspense continuity please write and let us know! I hope you pick up the rest of the series, as well as my debut book for Silhouette Nocturne next month (October 2007), entitled *Night Mischief*. That one will truly knock your socks off!

Take care and good reading,

Nina

Nina Bruhns

TOP-SECRET
BRIDE

Silhouette®
Romantic
SUSPENSE

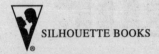 SILHOUETTE BOOKS

ISBN-13: 978-0-373-27550-2
ISBN-10: 0-373-27550-1

TOP-SECRET BRIDE

NINA BRUHNS

credits her Gypsy great-grandfather for her great love of adventure. She has lived and traveled all over the world, including a six-year stint in Sweden. She has been on scientific expeditions in places such as California, Spain, Egypt and the Sudan. Nina has two graduate degrees in archaeology, with a specialty in Egyptology. She speaks four languages and writes a mean hieroglyphics!

But Nina's first love has always been writing. For her, writing for Silhouette Books is the ultimate adventure. Drawing on her many experiences gives her stories a colorful dimension and allows her to create settings and characters out of the ordinary. She has won numerous awards for her previous titles, including a prestigious National Readers Choice Award, two Daphne du Maurier Awards of Excellence for Overall Best Romantic Suspense of the year, five Dorothy Parker Awards and two Golden Hearts Awards, among many others.

A native of Canada, Nina grew up in California and currently resides in Charleston, South Carolina, with her husband and three children. She loves to hear from her readers and can be reached at P.O. Box 2216, Summerville, SC 29484-2216, or by e-mail via her Web site at www.NinaBruhns.com or via the Harlequin Web site at www.eHarlequin.com.

To the members of the Charleston Author Society,
especially Tamar Myers and Mary Alice Monroe.
You ladies rock!

Chapter 1

Paris, France
September

Being here is insane.

SIS agent Marina Bond turned the key to one of the two rooms she'd hired for the afternoon in a seedy hotel in the Montmartre district of Paris, and carefully opened the door. You never knew what you'd find in these disgusting fleabag joints. But it was cheap, and the receptionist wouldn't remember her five minutes from now, even if she hadn't worn a black wig over her strawberry-blond hair.

After giving the small, threadbare room a swift visual inspection she went across the hall to the second room. "At least it's clean," Marina muttered.

And there was no way it could be bugged. She hadn't decided on the place until ten minutes ago. Two rooms might be overkill but, again, you never know.

She checked her watch. She must get this meeting over quickly, since she only had an hour lunch break. She'd gone awol in the middle of her current undercover operation, but she owed Corbett Lazlo. He'd saved her life once. The least she could do was return the favor.

There was a knock on the door. Rap, pause, rap-rap-rap.

The right pattern. Still, you couldn't be too careful. Marina drew her Glock 23 from her designer handbag, checked the door and grimaced. Why was there never a peephole when you needed one?

"Who is it?" she called.

"Corbett Lazlo sent me."

The muffled voice was male. British colonial—New Zealand? South Africa? Sounded distrustful. *And not Corbett.*

Her heartbeat kicked up. "Why didn't he come himself?"

"He's abroad at the moment. Sends his regrets. But you said this meeting was urgent, so here I am."

She scowled. "I just spoke to him on the phone last night. He was here, in Paris."

"Things happen fast in our business."

Did they ever. Marina worked for the Secret Intelligence Service—also widely known as MI6—the British equivalent of the American CIA. Corbett Lazlo was the owner and director of the Lazlo Group, one of the most elite private investigation agencies in the world. SIS used the group occasionally on ops. But could she trust that the disembodied male voice on the other side of the door was who he said he was?

"He also sends his regards to Moon Doggie," the voice said.

The shoulders of Marina's posh Givenchy trench notched down and a smile tugged at her lips. Moon Doggie, her father's code name in the U.S. Secret Service. She had met Corbett Lazlo years ago when she was a kid still living in the States before her parents' divorce, during one of her dad's protection gigs gone bad. Dad hated his Secret Service code name; only a select few were privy to it, including the man who'd saved his daughter from an uncertain fate. This guy was legit.

She lowered her weapon and eased open the door, motioning for the Lazlo agent to come in while she checked the hall. Empty.

Not that she expected to be followed. She'd been careful. She assumed he had, too, especially if he worked for Corbett Lazlo. But, yeah, you never knew.

Closing the door, she returned the Glock to her purse and turned to size up Corbett's stand-in. For a second she just stared, jolted by surprise.

The man was gorgeous. Upper thirties, tall—*very* tall—muscular, tanned with longish sun-streaked blond hair and a rakish mustache that accented an angled, character-filled face.

Eyes the color of the morning sky stared back at her. Assessingly.

"Agent Bond, I presume?" he asked, to his credit without a hint of amusement.

She nodded, keeping her own amusement to herself. Could she help it if Dad had gifted her with such a wildly inappropriate—or maybe wildly appropriate— last name? It had always been an open invitation for her colleagues to come up with all sorts of droll monikers and comical comments. Yeah, well, she'd never really minded. She could hold her own with ol' James.

The Lazlo agent grunted. "I'm—"

She cut him off before he could say his name. "Doesn't matter who you are."

"I'm von Kreus. DeWitt von Kreus," he completed firmly, tossing the leather jacket slung over one shoulder onto the bed. "Company policy to identify oneself."

His pronunciation was telling. Definitely South African. With a hint of Afrikaans. Her current undercover op was to infiltrate an African conflict diamond cartel. *Coincidence?* Her pulse jacked up again and she made a quick decision.

"Whatever. Take off your clothes," she ordered briskly.

His brows shot up. "Excuse me?"

"I'm invoking Denmark protocol," she said. "You've got a problem with that?"

"You think I'm *wired?*" Von Kreus's annoyance seemed genuine.

Denmark protocol was an old-school safety

measure only invoked these days as a last resort. In the field, when circumstances prevented electronic counterchecks, usually between potential enemies or rivals, stripping to the skin and changing venues eliminated your enemy's buddies listening in or taping the conversation.

"I'm not taking any chances," she stated evenly.

His jaw worked. "In that case, I won't take any, either. I invoke it in return."

She blinked. "What? Why?" He had no reason to suspect her of anything. He didn't even have to talk.

"If you don't like it you can always wait and speak to Lazlo himself," he said, noting her hesitation with a smirk of satisfaction. "The boss should be back in a day or two."

"This can't wait."

Corbett needed to hear this information asap. And she couldn't afford any more time off the grid. Besides, she wasn't shy. "Fine. Let's just get this over with," she muttered.

Quickly she unbuttoned her trench coat and laid it on the bed with her purse. Then she unbuttoned her silk blouse and peeled it off, too. It joined the other things, along with her black pageboy wig.

She tried to ignore him when he just stood there watching inscrutably as she removed the clip holding her blond hair in place and shook her head to loosen it from its confinement. His steady gaze followed the strands, then continued over her shoulders and down to her breasts where it lingered.

Her temper flared. "See anything you like?"

His pale-blue eyes darkened to steel and looked up at her with…hunger?

A sudden punch of awareness slammed through her insides, swift and sharp and just as hungry as his gaze. Damn, what was going on here?

Without replying, he pulled a SIG 226 Navy from the small of his back, then drew his black T-shirt over his head and pitched them both onto the bed next to his jacket, watching her the whole time with those icy-hot eyes.

She couldn't help it. She deliberately checked out his naked chest.

She wasn't disappointed. It was broad and buff and well defined, his nipples flat, dark and tight. Her own went pebble hard under her bra as she followed an arrow of sandy-colored hair to where it disappeared into the low-hipped band of his jeans.

Good Lord.

Crouching down, with rapid efficiency he removed his leather boots and his socks. Then he stood, crossed his arms and waited for her. To take off something else.

Sudden irrational gratitude flitted through her that her current undercover job required wearing designer clothes—and that she'd adopted the French habit of using self-tanner rather than unsexy pantyhose. She cleared her throat. And toed off her strappy sandals.

His brow raised mockingly when she stopped there.

Okay, fine. Whatever. Unzipping her pencil skirt, she added it to the growing pile on the bed. And gave her underwear a surreptitious glance. Pink, lacy and they matched. *Thank you, God.*

Von Kreus gave her expensive lingerie a more thorough inspection. As well as what lay under it. He seemed—

Aroused.

Heat scorched up her throat and cheeks as his body responded to his perusal with obvious approval. She swallowed a curse as, unfazed, he unbuckled his belt and slid out of his jeans. Then his boxer briefs were gone and he was standing in front of her completely naked.

Oh. My. God.

Make that *very* aroused.

Ignore it, she told herself, *and him,* and strove to remain calm as she removed the rest of her clothes. It was just a male body, for crying out loud. She was a cool, objective professional. This electricity sparking between them was not real. It was caused by hormones. Or pheromones. Or one of those other pesky chemical things that made people think and do inappropriate things at the most inappropriate times. And, anyway, men couldn't control when their equipment started to work. He was probably just as mortified as she at what was happening.

Except he didn't look mortified at all as she disposed of her last article of clothing. He looked… predatory.

A shiver coursed down her spine. It had been a long time since a man had looked at her like that. If ever. This man looked as if he wanted to eat her for breakfast.

And lunch.

And dinner.

She tore her gaze away from his. This wasn't what she'd come here for. As appealing as the thought suddenly was.

"Ear stud," she instructed, noticing the glint of gold in his left lobe. Trying desperately to stay on task.

He took it off without protest. While he did, she removed her own jewelry, then pulled in a deep breath, went to the door and checked out the hallway. All clear.

"Lock up and come with me," she told him. Scooting quickly across the hall to the second room she'd rented, she waited for him to join her, then locked the door behind him.

"Aren't you being a bit paranoid?" he asked, flipping the key to the first room onto the nightstand.

"I'm here because of Corbett. But I don't want this favor to come back and bite me in the butt."

Damn. Bad choice of words. She fought another flush that threatened to creep up her neck.

Von Kreus tipped his head and spread his arms out wide. "Body search?" The ghost of a challenge passed through his expression.

Far too tempting.

"That won't be necessary," she assured him. He clearly hadn't expected the Denmark protocol, so he wouldn't have hidden a bug that thoroughly on his person. Switching rooms would take care of anything planted in his clothes. Besides, despite his African connection, instinct told her he had no hidden agenda.

Her decision had nothing whatsoever to do with her not wanting to touch the man's awesome body.

"All right, then." He stood still, obviously waiting for her to come closer.

As per the protocol. Which she'd never actually had to use before. She'd learned the outdated maneuver in one of her induction training courses, amidst massive snickering and lewd jokes from the other, mainly male, recruits. That had been eight years ago. Why, oh, why hadn't she learned her lesson from their reaction?

But she had no choice. She'd started this.

"All right, then," she echoed, and walked right up to him as though she'd done this every day of her beloved SIS career.

But she was distracted. And she ended up too close to him. *Way* too close. Close like she-could-feel-his-curly-chest-hair-tickle-her-nipples-and-his-warm-breath-in-her-hair close. Not to mention—

Oh, God. This was not good.

He bent his mouth to her ear, bringing them within a hair's breadth. Less, in some places. A lot less. Goose bumps shimmered over her whole body.

"Now, what was so important that I had to strip naked to hear it?" he softly taunted in his honey-and-gravel accent.

He had to know what he was doing to her. How her body was reacting to his nearness. That was the only explanation for his sexy-as-sin, deep, silky whisper. And the fact that he allowed various body parts to brush provocatively against hers.

She closed her eyes, wanting to stop at least the visual stimulation. But she was immediately filled with the male scent of him. Spicy. Masculine.

Arousing. And felt his hard flesh against her as he adjusted his stance. Closer still.

Desperation added its bite to the adrenaline already rushing through her. What had gotten into her today? She never acted like this. Her body never rebelled against her good sense like this. But face it, she had never been this attracted to a man before. Or this quickly. In all her years on the job, much of them undercover, she had never been as… tempted…to throw caution to the wind.

Think of Corbett, she told herself. Corbett was why she was here, enduring this crazy situation, instead of running as far and as fast as she could.

She pulled herself together. Keeping her voice low, striving to be businesslike, she spoke past the tightness in her throat. "There's someone out there making threats against the Lazlo Group."

Von Kreus's eyes sharpened, suddenly focused. His soft reply clipped out, "Who?"

"I don't know. I'm currently working under-cover and—"

"On what?" he demanded, grasping her wrist with his fingers. He gazed at her intently. It was worse than the predatory look he'd had earlier. It felt like he was aiming a laser sight at her.

She shook it off. "You know I can't tell you that."

He didn't look pleased but gave a nod. "For now." But he didn't let go of her wrist. "Go on."

"There's a man named Abayomi Camara—"

"The Angolan?"

"How did you—"

"I'm from South Africa. What about him?"

"Abayomi Camara is currently in France. SIS suspects he is a broker for several African terrorist groups, trafficking illegal conflict diamonds in exchange for firearms."

"Right. He runs the biggest blood diamond cartel in Angola." His eyes narrowed. "But why would he threaten the Lazlo Group?"

"He didn't, exactly. My cover involves working at a jewelry boutique, which he occasionally frequents. He was there yesterday and I happened to overhear a private mobile phone conversation between him and someone I assume is one of his European contacts. They were talking about a recent incident, a bombing in Rome. The Lazlo Group headquarters there, I believe."

He stared at her and frowned. "*Yessus.* One of our agents was killed in that bombing, along with—" his jaw set "—a courier named Kruger who dealt in conflict diamonds. They were both shot execution-style, then the building bombed, probably to cover up the murders. What exactly did Camara say on the phone?"

"He said 'Not a problem. You saved me the trouble of killing the thief myself,' then the other person said something, and Camara said 'Believe me, everyone's life will be much easier without the Lazlo outfit sticking their noses where they don't belong. Best of luck removing them all.'"

"So it was Camara the courier worked for. We never did find out that bit of information." Von

Kreus's fingers tightened around Marina's wrist as his jaw muscles went rigid. "Do you have any idea who Camara was talking to?"

She shook her head. "Sorry. I was somewhere I wasn't supposed to be, listening to a conversation I shouldn't have been listening to."

"Understood. Do you happen to have a phone number for Camara? I could check the call records."

"It was one of those purple disposable cell phones. Untraceable. Only good within Europe. But he was speaking English."

"Not much to go on. Anything else?"

"It sounded like they've been working together for a while. He used terms like 'the usual place' and 'the usual arrangements.' I think the other person must have been someone fairly high up the food chain. The way Camara spoke was familiar but quite deferential."

The South African's steel-blue eyes bored into her. "And you can't think of any way to find out who it was?"

"I'm sorry. I hope Corbett can somehow track them down. It's why I called."

She dropped her gaze to her wrist, which the agent—Von Kreus—still held as he silently considered what she'd told him. She tried to shake it loose. No luck. When she looked up again, she realized she could no longer see his face. He'd moved so close his chin was pressed to her head above her ear. All at once she felt his other hand—resting on her hip. Lightly, as though he'd put it there unconsciously.

But she was fully conscious of it. Of him. Of

their bodies pressed together. Suddenly it was all she could think of.

Another megadose of sexual awareness rocketed through her. She felt her breasts pillow into his chest and his arousal pulse, felt the muscles of his thighs flex taut and hard against hers. Everywhere his flesh touched her skin it burned like hot silk.

"Can you get me a list of which terrorist groups SIS thinks might be dealing with Abayomi Camara?" he asked. "We're especially interested in an organization run by the Dumont family. I believe SIS calls it by the nickname SNAKE."

She tried to concentrate. Truly. And to answer him. But her mouth had gone so dry she couldn't even get out a squeak. In panic, she nodded instead.

Big mistake. The movement drew attention to their position….

She could tell the exact moment when his conscious awareness of her body returned. His steady breathing stopped abruptly. A few seconds later it started up again, a shade quicker. His fingers curled a shade tighter over her hip and wrist. His arousal grew a shade thicker and harder against her belly.

If she didn't move immediately, she was going to… He was going to…

She jerked away from him. Out of his grasp. Distancing herself from the temptation of his impressive, excruciatingly male body. Her own was in a frenzy. Every cell cried out in protest at being yanked away from him.

"I'll e-mail that list to Corbett," she managed to

say with only one small crack in her voice. Then she turned and fled.

She got as far as the door.

His hand slapped it shut as she struggled to get it open, and he held it firmly closed against her feeble attempt to pull at the knob. Every marshal arts move she'd ever learned flew out the window as a sense of inevitability overwhelmed her.

He didn't say anything. Just grasped her arm and swung her to face him, pushing her back against the door. She felt his hand gather her hair and wind it around his palm so she couldn't move her head.

Then his lips came down on hers.

Her whole body electrified as he took her in a hard, bruising kiss, his tongue thrusting between her teeth at her gasp of surprise.

The erotic feel of his hair-smattered skin as it rubbed provocatively against hers made her dizzy with want. She wanted more of him. Closer. Harder. She wound her arms about his neck and pulled him down to her. A growling noise rumbled deep in his throat at her moan of pleasure. His hand in her hair tightened. The other one smoothed from her hip up to her waist and back down.

She groaned. He deepened the kiss.

It went on and on and on.

He tasted so good. Felt so good. She wanted more, more, more.

He was driving her mad with need. She wanted to crawl up his tall, hard body and wrap herself around him until he—

His fingers slid between her legs and she cried out. *Yes. Until he did that.*

She whimpered. Sucked in a breath. Moaned again as he touched her. *There!* And gave herself up to the exquisite pleasure of his fingertips as they coaxed her fire into a burning conflagration.

"That's right, Marina," he whispered as she began to tremble and quiver. "Let me take you there."

He remembered her first name. "What's your—"

"Shh," he murmured. "It's Witt," he said, and covered her mouth with his.

Witt. It was the last coherent thought she had. Then all she could do was moan it over and over as his passionate tongue and his clever fingers swiftly made her forget her own name.

Except he kept reminding her. Murmured between whispered endearments and hoarse erotic demands.

A sudden climax jolted through her body, sweeping over her with a drenching slam of pleasure. He caught her scream in his throat and fed it back to her as a feral growl as he shoved his knees between her thighs, spread them, and with a guttural cry impaled himself deep inside her. Her climax prismed and exploded into a million brilliant colors.

She drowned in the taste of him. And the taste of wild desire as they ate at each other, merging their bodies in reckless need. She couldn't see; she couldn't hear. But she could feel—Witt's body thrusting into her, the awesome power of his lust for her, the strength of her own for him. The scintillatingly perfect physical joining.

And then they were both hurtling over the edge. Sharp, almost painful pleasure. Rough voices calling out together. Hot liquid pulsing deep inside.

His mouth…his mouth lingered on her as though he didn't want it to stop any more than she did. She wished it could go on and on forever, this rush of goodness and delight she was feeling in the arms of a stranger.

But eventually the throbbing rhythm slowed and his lips tore from hers. Her leaden legs slipped down his hips and he twisted around so his back was against the door.

"*Yerre,* woman," he muttered under his panting breath, still holding her tight so thankfully she couldn't completely melt into a puddle. "*Eish,* what you do to me."

She couldn't recall having done a whole lot of anything; it had all been him. The man was…amazing.

"The feeling," she managed, barely, "is mutual." Her heart was beating so fast she couldn't understand why she felt like fading away from lethargy. She didn't want to move. Not ever.

His breath stirred her hair as he leaned down and whispered, "More. I want more of you." His hands caressed her backside.

She hummed her agreement, a smile invading her whole being. "Yes, please."

She would gladly give him as much of herself as he wanted. She'd spend the next hour in bed with him. The next five hours. Hell, the next five days. There was nothing and nowhere she'd rather be—

Damn!

No!

She jerked out of her sexual haze with a start. What time was it? What the hell was she *doing?* She couldn't be here! *She had to get back on the grid.*

"Babe, what's wrong?" Witt looked down at her with a frown.

She pulled out of his arms, horrified that she'd let herself get so completely sidetracked. That she'd let herself— "I'm sorry. I…I have to go."

She ducked into the bathroom for a minute. When she came out he hadn't moved, his back still against the door. His arms were crossed and his face a stony mask. Was this cold man the same one with whom she had just shared the hottest, most-intense minutes of her life?

"I want to see you again," he said. He still wasn't smiling. And he wasn't letting her through the door.

An unwilling thrill spun through her. He looked dangerous. He sounded dangerous. The very air around him felt dangerous. And yet, all that danger was directed at wanting her.

This was something new. Oh, men had come on to her plenty. They'd said they wanted her, but she knew sex was what they really wanted. Sometimes she'd even given it to them. But this was different. This *man* was different. Yeah, he wanted sex. But seeing the determined way he was regarding her, she was dead certain he wanted sex with *her.* Marina Bond. And "no" wasn't going to be an option.

Unfortunately, "no" was the only answer she could give. And he was just going to have to live with it.

"Believe me, I wish that were possible," she told him as she grabbed the key from the bedside table. "But you know who I work for. I can't—" She shook her head. "It's not going to happen."

"We'll see," he said, and pushed off the door. He clasped her arm as she reached for the knob. "My name is DeWitt von Kreus, in case you've forgotten, and I have a level-one security clearance with SIS. Check me out. No one's going to care if we're sleeping together."

"I'll care. I'm in the middle of an op and I need my full concentration on it."

After a tension-filled second, he gritted his teeth and let her go. She opened the door and peeked into the hall to make sure it was empty before crossing back to the other room. She needed her clothes and her gun and then to get the hell out of there.

Before she did something really stupid. Like give him her phone number.

He stalked after her and they dressed wordlessly, the air between them crackling as if they were dancing between downed power wires.

"Ready?" she asked, adjusting her black wig. He gave a curt nod as he jammed his SIG into his waistband. Time to go. But she didn't want to leave things like this between them. It had been...good.

"Witt," she said. "It was amazing. Unexpected but amazing. Under any other circumstances..."

She let her words trail off. No sense making empty promises. Her world, her job, didn't allow for more than they'd already had. And even if it did, she wasn't interested. She'd seen firsthand the heartache her parents had gone through when they'd tried to mix love and danger. No, thanks.

Witt's ice-blue eyes revealed nothing, but as she reached for the doorknob, his palm wrapped around her jaw and he pulled her face to his for a last, searing kiss.

"This isn't over," he said, and let her go.

Her heartbeat went into triple time. But he made no further comment, nor move toward her. She took a deep breath and forged through the door. His light bootfalls followed her as she clacked down the dingy staircase, past the shabby reception desk and out into the blinding Paris sun.

As soon as they hit the sidewalk, a muffled *pop* echoed off the quiet walls of the neighborhood. They both froze. Next to Marina's foot, a cobble-stone exploded.

Another *pop* sounded. And Witt growled a curse. *Bloody hell.* Someone was shooting at them!

Chapter 2

Stinging pain razored through Witt's bicep. Bright-crimson rivulets ran down his hand from under the cuff of his leather jacket. *Yessus.* He ignored the pain and grabbed Marina, shoving her back into the hotel doorway.

"My God, you're hit," she muttered, frowning at the blood and the two neat holes in his upper sleeve.

"My favorite jacket," he gritted, peering out from the archway. "The little shit's going to pay." He shook the sleeve off his arm and whipped a handkerchief from his pocket.

She took it from him, binding his wound as he tried to spot the shooter. "He must be using a silencer," she said. "Do you see him?"

"No." They were in an area typical of this section of Paris. Short, narrow lanes bisected other short, narrow lanes in a confused tangle. It was easy to get lost and impossible to see more than a few dozen meters in either direction. "He could be anywhere."

Marina pulled the snub-nosed Glock automatic from her purse. "You go left. I'll go right," she said, and started to take off.

Whoa! He grabbed her arm and jerked her back, just as another hole was drilled into the brick next to the doorway. "Are you *bos*—crazy? You can't go out there."

She yanked at her arm. "Let me go! We need to take this idiot down before he hurts somebody."

He didn't think so. He pushed her as far into the alcove as she'd fit. "Yeah, including you. Stay here. I'll go."

She snorted. "Like hell. I do this for a living, von Kreus, remember?"

Hands on his hips, he scowled pointedly at her fancy attire. "You always chase bad guys in high heels?"

She glowered back at him. "No. Sometimes they're wearing boots."

For a split second anger spiked at her cheekiness. Then a grin suddenly broke through. Damn, he liked his women a little sassy. Made things a hell of a lot more interesting. "Stroppy little cherrie, aren't you?" he murmured.

"I have no idea what that means, but your lame macho posturing is letting the shooter get away."

She raised her weapon and ducked out of the sheltering doorway at a crouched run.

"Damn it, girl, wait!" He took off after her.

She made an alternate suggestion. Which just made him grin wider.

More shots followed them, nipping at their shadows. That wiped the smile from his face. "Who's shooting at you, Marina?" he called just loud enough for her to hear.

"Me? You're the one bleeding!" she called back.

He caught up to her and forcibly hauled her into another doorway. Another shot trailed them. This was getting ridiculous. "No one knows I'm here. Who wants you dead?"

Her breath came in short pants as she shrugged. "Let me count the terrorists."

Her and him, both. He wondered if she had a price on her head, too. "Anyone get out of jail recently?"

"No." She took a deep breath and slipped out of the alcove again. "I'd have been notified."

Giving up, he ran in tandem with her, each taking turns covering the other from doorways along the street. He had to admit, she was doing a hell of a job in those heels. Her ankles didn't even wobble.

With a curse, he redirected his gaze from her ankles to the street. "Could you have blown your current cover?" he called.

"Trust me," she called back, "the people I'm dealing with wouldn't have missed. It must be you this guy's after."

More shots came in a volley. They both slammed into the next alcove together, breathing hard.

"Like I said, no one except Corbett Lazlo knew I was meeting you," he said. "And I wasn't followed. I made damn sure of that."

Her eyes carefully scanned the street and the buildings across from them. "What about Camara's phone conversation? Could this attack have something to do with the vendetta against the Lazlo Group?"

Witt thought about that as he peeked out from their hiding place. Theoretically, it wasn't outside the realm of possibility. Someone really seemed to have it in for the Lazlo Group. Three of their agents had already been killed under suspicious circumstances, and another killed during the Rome attack. And now the phone call. But...

"Logistically, I don't see how," he concluded, cautiously leaning out to check the sidewalk in both directions, weapon at the ready. There were no more shots. "But I'll certainly report it to Corbett when I give him your information."

"There!" she said, pointing to a man, blond, just under six feet tall, running for a city bus at the end of the block.

Witt started to give chase, but stopped when he got a better look. "Hell, that's just a kid. Nineteen, twenty max."

"Tell that to bin Laden," she muttered, coming up alongside him.

She was right, of course. Terrorists were getting younger every day. He himself had seen children as young as seven or eight wielding machine guns in some countries. But unfortunately, there was no chance they'd catch this bus. It was pulling away from the curb several hundred meters away.

Tucking his weapon back into his waistband, Witt whipped out his mobile phone and snapped a photo of the kid through the window before the bus disappeared around the corner. "I'll run this past our facial-recognition software, see if anyone pops." He turned to her. "Meanwhile, you better come with me."

She balked, dropping her Glock back into her purse. "I'm only on lunch break. I have to get back."

"The hell you do. Come on." He grabbed her hand firmly and didn't let go.

Two seconds later he had his cheek pressed up against the rough bricks of the building, her knee up his butt and his arm yanked high behind his back. It hurt. Just a little. Luckily it wasn't the arm with the bleeding gunshot wound.

"Impressive," he said to the bricks. He'd have to remember this in the future.

Four seconds later he'd reversed their positions and she was pressed against the wall. In handcuffs.

"But not impressive enough," he whispered in her ear.

"Brute," she hissed.

"Who, me, *skat?*"

"Stop using words I don't understand."

"*Skat?* It means treasure," he murmured. "Something a man calls his woman."

"I am so not your woman, Witt. Take these cuffs off me at once!"

He felt a sudden, unreasonable and totally unexpected need to prove her wrong. She might not know it yet, but she *was* his. And with her in handcuffs, he could easily—

Herre yessus.

Because of his background, he'd never found the idea of bondage the least bit arousing. Quite the opposite. But seeing Marina with her big green eyes, her plump kissable lips, her round bottom nicely defined even under her belted trench coat—and those damned sexy high heels—all locked up in his handcuffs... *Yerre,* his body was slammed by a powerful punch of desire. It recalled in vivid detail what it had so recently done to her in that hotel room. It wanted to do it again.

Now.

"Back off, von Kreus," she growled.

He whipped her around to face him. "That's not what you were saying a few minutes ago, *liefde.*" He gave her a knowing look. "Yeah. That means lover."

There were dark flags of red on her cheeks, and her breath came fast and shallow. It could have been from running. In an alternate universe.

He stepped into her, pressing his body against hers, and took. He covered her mouth and thrust his tongue between her lips, claiming what she was so frustratingly reluctant to give. As he'd done in the hotel room. And just as she'd done then, she moaned, opening to him.

She wanted him as much as he wanted her. Her whole body shouted her desire. So, why the reluctance?

"I have to go," she said, tearing her lips from his.

"When can I see you again?"

"I told you it's impossible."

"Why? You want me."

"I can't afford the distraction. You know how this job is. One slip-up and I'm dead. Maybe we can talk when the op is over."

Not good enough. He didn't want to wait a month or a week or even a day. And frankly, he was worried about her safety. The shooting had been directed at her; he was sure of it. If her cover was blown, she would be dead with or without a distraction.

"Bring me in on the op," he said. "The Lazlo Group works with SIS all the time. I could—"

"What? No! I don't need your help. Now take these things off me. I mean it, Witt."

DeWitt von Kreus was an interrogator by profession. *What* he was. *Who* he was. Which meant he knew instinctively when to step back and give the subject some space. Establish some trust. Afterward, he could move back in for the kill. Later, when they least expected it. When *she* least expected it.

"Whatever." He turned her and undid the cuffs. "I have my car. I'll drive you so you won't be late."

She looked at him, hesitant. Wary. Then she nodded. "Thanks."

It was less than a ten-minute drive down the hill

to the chic shopping district between Blvd Haussmann and Blvd de la Madeleine where Marina asked to be let off.

"I'll hang around for a while," Witt said, pulling his Land Rover to the curb. "If you suspect your cover is blown, get out of there fast. I'll have your back."

She gave him a tolerant smile. "I'm a big girl, von Kreus. I'll be fine on my own. But I appreciate the offer."

He could tell she really didn't appreciate it. She was just being polite. That annoyed him to no end. He'd rather she just tell him to go to hell. Not that he'd leave. He just didn't like being patronized.

With a last look over her shoulder, Marina walked into a glitzy boutique called Glace Chaud, the front window overflowing with gold, silver and diamonds. She'd said her undercover gig involved working in a jewelry store. If the boutique Glace Chaud was involved with Abayomi Camara and illegal conflict diamonds, she *could* be in huge danger. Camara's cartel was notoriously ruthless and vicious. They didn't call them blood diamonds for nothing. Witt had to admit she was right about one thing. If it had been Camara's people shooting, he and Marina would be pushing up daisies.

He stewed for several long minutes, watching to make sure she didn't come running out of the place, gun blazing. Then he called Corbett.

"Yooit, boikie," his boss greeted him. Corbett found some perverse amusement learning bits of in-

appropriate South African slang and trying it out on Witt. *"Hoesit?"* Which meant, roughly, hey, how's it going, boyo?

The slang was so atypical of the somewhat formal and refined Corbett Lazlo, Witt couldn't help but laugh. "No fine *bru,*" he replied, playing along. Just fine.

"Huh?"

"Give it up, boss. You'll never grasp the subtleties."

Corbett sighed and got down to business. "So how'd the meet with Marina Bond go?"

"That's what I'm calling about. You back in town?"

"On the jet. Landing in an hour."

"We have a problem." Witt relayed everything that Marina had told him about the overheard phone conversation.

Corbett swore softly. "So that would seem to confirm a vendetta against the Lazlo Group."

"Looks that way," Witt said. "That e-mail you got last week implied as much. This information does seem to clinch it."

Corbett had received a series of threatening e-mails during the previous weeks. The last one had said, "Think you know what's going on? Think again." The head of the Group's IT department, Lucia Cordez, had been trying to trace the origin of the messages, but so far unsuccessfully.

"You think whoever Camara was talking to could be the same person sending those e-mails?" Corbett mused.

"Very possible. Randy Kruger, the man who was

executed along with our agent in Rome, was a conflict diamond courier," Witt reminded him. "Unless you think that connection is a coincidence?"

"You know I don't believe in coincidences," Corbett said grimly. "Mitch Llama, our agent who was trying to interrogate Kruger, believes Kruger had a contact other than Jared Williams within SIS. Someone high up."

Witt knew that Chloe Winchester, second in command of the Lazlo Group IT department, had been caught feeding sensitive and confidential information about Lazlo agents to Williams, a low-level SIS agent. She had been fired and Williams arrested, but he refused to say for which of his SIS superiors he'd been illegally spying on the Lazlo Group. The list of possible suspects was short but illustrious, including several section chiefs and even a deputy director of SIS. Ferreting out the culprit without raising an uproar would be very tricky.

Corbett pushed out a breath. "Unfortunately we could never connect Chloe or Williams to the Rome bombing, or any of the other assassinations. And Kruger's only provable connection with it all was that he was killed along with our agent. It *could* be just one bizarre coincidence."

"Supported by the fact that none of them seem to have any real motive for pursuing this kind of vicious vendetta against the Lazlo Group," Witt said, feeling a spurt of frustration. "Why would anyone at SIS want to see you ruined and your agents dead?"

Corbett was silent for a moment. "You know MI6—SIS—and I have a history."

"Sure. You started your career there. Then they accused you of treason and tossed you out. But you were subsequently exonerated of all wrongdoing. And we work joint operations with them all the time now! Surely that ancient history can't have anything to do with this?"

"Mitch Llama thinks it could."

Witt remembered discussing all these tentative connections and theories with Mitch and Corbett last month.

"His professional-jealousy theory? That you were completely ruined but rebounded to become richer and more powerful than your accusers, thus making someone furious enough to kill you?" Witt shrugged. "It's possible, I suppose."

"Does sound a bit far-fetched, even to me," Corbett admitted. They both fell silent for a moment. "And I truly don't want to believe anyone high up in the SIS can be involved in any of this. I can't imagine a high-ranking British official dealing in blood diamonds and murder, regardless of motive. But again, I don't believe in coincidence."

Witt agreed. The evidence, though a bit circumstantial, was damning. "Didn't you work with some of the men on our suspect list? In the old days I mean? Deputy Director Roland Milleflora for instance. Wasn't he Head of Section in Rome when we opened our headquarters there?"

"Yes," Corbett admitted reluctantly. There was a

pause, then he added, "And as much as I dislike the whole sordid business, I've already arranged for a couple of agents to investigate those connections."

Corbett had his determined voice on. The boss defended his own, and this threat to them triggered a vicious, relentlessly protective fury Witt was glad he was on the right side of.

"Is there any way for Marina to find out who Abayomi Camara was talking to?" Corbett asked, bringing the conversation back around to the present dilemma of the phone conversation.

"She says no," Witt said. "She's worried about jeopardizing her current mission by asking around. But there's more."

Witt told his boss about the shooting at the hotel.

"You were *shot?*" Corbett's alarm was palpable.

"In the arm. Just a nick. Honestly? Despite everything we just talked about, I think the shooter was going for Marina." Witt listed all his reasons, the major one being that no one knew he'd be meeting her—it was supposed to have been Corbett—therefore the shooter must have tracked Marina to the meet.

"And not a professional hit?"

"Not in my opinion. But that doesn't mean whoever it was won't try for her again."

"Or you, if you're wrong about the target. Bloody hell, man, either way is bad news. I'll send a forensic crew to collect the evidence from the street. From what you say there should be a half-dozen bullets lodged in the buildings and hopefully as many casings on the ground. Maybe we'll get lucky and can trace the ballistics."

"Let's hope."

Corbett swore softly again. "Marina's father is a good friend of mine, Witt. If I've somehow involved her in more danger…"

It was that loyalty thing again. "Well, I have an idea," Witt said.

"Tell me."

"Since Marina was eavesdropping on Abayomi Camara, it's pretty clear her mission has something to do with the African conflict diamond trade. Which in turn seems to have a possible connection with the threats against the Lazlo Group. I suggest coordinating with SIS and sending me in with her, undercover."

"Keep talking."

"I can work the vendetta angle under the guise of helping Marina with her assignment. My past association with the South African anti-apartheid movement will give me juice with Camara and the rebels he's supplying with arms. He'll be impressed that I sided with the ANC and that my own people have put a price on my head."

"How do you propose setting things up?"

"I could go in as a security guard at Glace Chaud, the jewelry store. Camara must be in Paris to arrange a delivery of rough diamonds. He'll have bodyguards. I can get to know them easier than Marina. I speak their language. And they'll trust me because they'll think I'm on their side."

Corbett made his decision quickly. "Sounds workable. Let's run with it."

"How fast can you get me in?"

"The British Prime Minister believes we can do no wrong after we rescued his kidnapped daughter two months ago. He'll make the necessary phone call to SIS and the French authorities. An hour, tops. Where are you now?"

"Keeping an eye on Marina." Witt gave him the address of Glace Chaud.

"I'll contact the store's security company and make them an offer they can't refuse. By the time we get official clearance, the regular security guard will be pulled, due to a fabricated family emergency."

"Best not to tell the store manager why I'm there," Witt suggested. "Wouldn't want to interfere in Marina's op."

"Right. And if he's involved, he shouldn't be suspicious of you, since you'll be sent by his regular security company."

"I'll need a change of clothes," Witt said, glancing down at his outfit. "Upscale. And some extra firepower." He grimaced. "Oh, and maybe a Band-Aid for the arm."

"Sit tight," Corbett said, and rang off. The boss wasn't much for idle chitchat. Which was fine. Neither was Witt.

But Corbett was a whiz at getting things done in record time. Exactly forty-nine minutes later, Witt was walking through the front door of Glace Chaud wearing a three-thousand-euro Yves St. Laurent suit, shirt and tie, thousand-euro Prada boots, a five-hundred-euro Bianchi leather shoulder holster for his SIG Navy, carrying a Walther P99 tucked at the small of his back and a Beretta Tomcat in a specially designed boot holster. Yeah, and his arm was cleaned, stitched and neatly plastered.

When he strode into the boutique, Marina was standing behind a display case helping a couple pick out a ring. She looked up. He smiled broadly. Her jaw dropped.

The manager hurried over to him. "May I help you *monsieur?*" he asked in French.

"*Oui,*" Witt answered, his eyes never leaving Marina. "DeWitt von Kreus is the name," he said, pulling out a sheaf of credentials from the security company and handing them to the man. "I'm your replacement security guard."

This was a beaut of a setup. Witt had been between jobs a few weeks now and had been getting antsy for some action. The boss was obviously worried about the escalating threats to the Lazlo Group. With this mission Witt would be killing two birds with one stone. Three, if you counted his plans for Marina.

However, Witt's new lover was not a happy camper. In fact, he figured if she had anything to say about it, he wouldn't be coming within twenty meters of her anytime soon.

Of course, she didn't have anything to say about it. It wasn't that Witt was egotistical or overbearing or controlling or anything, it was just—

Okay, maybe he was all of those things. He wanted her, badly, so he'd have her. End of discussion. But she wanted him, too, so that made things a bit easier. He just had to show her how little her objections meant in the grand scheme.

It wasn't as though he wanted to marry the woman. He was just talking sex, here. He knew she had her priorities, and her job topped the list. Same for him. No conflict there. But healthy adults needed sex. He and Marina did it well together, and they were in the same business so they understood each other. What was the harm? Sex wasn't a distraction. It *prevented* distractions.

But judging by the veiled dagger looks she'd been giving him all afternoon, she didn't agree. Witt figured he'd better keep his distance for a while.

The store's manager, Monsieur Henri, was not particularly happy, either, at having his old and trusted security guard replaced at a moment's notice with a new guy. He showed Witt around the store with barely concealed resentment, but he didn't appear suspicious of any ulterior reasons for the switch. Witt just smiled and nodded and memorized the floor plan. Midsize showroom in front lined with glass cases, one door to the back where two offices, a tiny lunch room, restroom and a walk-in double-locking vault were situated. Only one outside entrance, in front. That could prove tricky.

It turned out Witt's duties as security guard included opening doors for customers, hailing taxis, checking packages and generally keeping watch, in addition to having a finger on the trigger in case of a robbery. There was an actual doorman, Claude, who did most of the grunt stuff, and they worked as a team. After an hour, they were like a well-oiled greeting machine. Witt could play the charming flirt with the best of them. Little old ladies watch out. Claude was big and black with a broad, toothy smile. He was from the Congo. The Congo was one of the major players in the illegal conflict-diamond trade. Nothing like being obvious.

By closing time, he and Claude were old friends. Witt hadn't mentioned his antiapartheid work or ANC connections, but had revealed enough information about his background that whomever Claude was reporting to—presumably Camara—could find out everything there was to know about DeWitt von Kreus. Everything that the Lazlo Group deliberately kept active on the Internet. It was all true. It was the subsequent decade-long hunt for him by the Afrikaans—or Dutch South African—nationalists that had been slightly exaggerated. Bad guys trusted you more if someone wanted you dead badly enough to pay a lot of money for someone to do it. And they treated you with a hell of a lot more respect if they thought the reason you were being hunted was that you had tortured top-secret information out of your own people, then killed them.

Of course, he hadn't tortured or killed anyone. He hadn't needed to. He was just that good at his vocation. And after they'd spilled their guts to the enemy, most of his interrogees were happy to disappear all on their own, with only a little encouragement.

Anyway, Claude would report all this to Camara, and Witt would be in like Flint with the bad guys.

The good guys—well, girl—however, was a different story.

Marina deliberately ignored him for the entire afternoon, right up until she was walking out the door after closing time. She was the last salesgirl to leave; the manager followed her.

Witt snagged Marina's wrist as she strode past him. "We need to talk."

Claude glanced at them in surprise. "You two know each other?"

Witt banded his arm around her. "Oh, yeah. We know each other quite well. Marina is my fiancée." He was as surprised as she was at that last bit. But damn if he didn't like the idea.

Her eyes bugged and her mouth opened, then snapped shut. "I told you I didn't want to see you again," she said through clenched teeth. *"Ever."*

Witt shot Claude a wink, cozying up to the role. "Lover's tiff." He pressed a kiss onto Marina's black pageboy wig, ignoring her attempt to pry herself loose from him. "Now, *skat,* I know you don't mean that. Come on. I'll give you a ride home."

"I'll walk, thank you," she said between her teeth.

"Beauty," he said. "The Land Rover is right out front." While she was confused, he led her out the door, then stopped to watch Monsieur Henri lock up for the night. "Remember what happened last time," he warned her under his breath when it felt like she might try something stupid. "And, yes, I do have handcuffs."

The manager lowered a security frame of steel bars over the storefront and snapped the heavy padlock shut. Claude waggled his eyebrows and Monsieur Henri gave him a scowl before the two headed off to the nearest Métro stop, leaving Witt and Marina standing on their own.

"Come on," he said, tugging her arm. "How about some dinner?"

She dug in her heels. "Hello? *Fiancée?* Are you crazy?"

"Nice touch, hey?"

"No! And you have a serious problem if you think I'm going anywh—"

"What are you afraid of, Marina?"

She looked at him askance. "What? Nothing! I can—"

He held up a hand. "I know, I know. You can take care of yourself."

She glared. "That's right, and—"

"I'm not asking to take care of you. I'm just asking you to dinner."

"Yeah, sure. And what else?" It wasn't really a question. More of a derisive statement.

He gave her his most disarming smile and answered anyway. "Only what you want to give me."

Her eyes rolled along with her stomach. He grinned. "Are you always this obnoxious?" she muttered.

"Nah. I'm on my best behavior."

She sighed, a sign she was close to capitulating. "You realize I'm pissed as hell at you."

"I got that."

"I don't want or need your help on this op. I could kill you for horning in on it."

"Hopefully it won't come to that."

She huffed. "And that fiancée thing? Witt, this morning was a mistake. A huge mistake. I don't want a fiancé, or a boyfriend, or a playmate, or a relationship of any kind."

"What about just friends?"

"Oh, please."

His grin widened. "Just good friends?"

She ground her teeth and poked him in the chest. "See? That's exactly what I'm talking about."

"Me, too, *skat,*" he said, and slung an arm around her shoulders, guiding her up the sidewalk to his car.

"I can't believe you told them we're engaged. It's too convenient. They're going to smell a setup."

This was good. She was already thinking of him as part of the op. "We'll see."

"They'll never trust me now. Damn! How are we going to explain this?"

He wasn't too worried. "We can iron out the details later. I'm starving. Somehow I managed to skip lunch." He unlocked the door and handed her in before she had a chance to protest that, too. "I know this great place in the Latin Quarter. A bit touristy, but the fondue is to die for." She still had that stubborn expression. "Nutella-banana dessert crepes…" he tempted.

She threw up her hands. "Okay. I give up. I'll have dinner with you. But that's it. Nothing else."

He smiled inwardly as he revved the engine. See? No one could resist him. He was irresistible.

Now all he had to do was convince her of how ir-resistible *she* was.

And that all this resisting was just plain counter-productive.

It took Witt three days to get close enough to kiss Marina.

Even the bad guys trusted him faster than she did. Claude must have done his homework, because the morning of Witt's second day at Glace Chaud the doorman greeted him like a long-lost cousin.

"Should have told me you are a brother in arms," he said in his melodic Congolese accent, clapping Witt on the back.

Marina watched them from behind the jewelry counter, trying not to appear curious.

"That was ages ago," Witt said with a shrug. "I live in Paris now. It's a long way from the Transvaal."

"But your heart is still in Africa," Claude said quietly, squeezing his shoulder as if he understood.

For a second it felt like Claude was squeezing Witt's heart. It was so very true. Witt missed his homeland with a fierce longing. Not for the reasons the other man thought. But because of the poignant memories. Of the farm where he'd spent his happy childhood. Of his good friends, black and white. Of his dear mother and father, whom he hadn't seen in ten long years. Of Sarah, before…

"Yes, I'll always miss Africa," Witt confessed softly. Then he gathered himself and winked at Marina, who was still watching them. "But Paris does have its compensations."

Claude chuckled as he followed Witt's gaze. "She's a pretty little thing," he said. "A bit buttoned-up for my taste…."

"You've never seen her in action, my friend," Witt said with a grin.

Since Claude had seen them leave together last night Witt let him draw his own conclusions. Wrong, as it happened. More's the pity.

But Witt worked his charm on Marina for that day and the next, and finally cornered her alone in the walk-in vault the afternoon of their third day. He was supposed to be watching her fetch a tray of emerald rings. She was bending over to pull a drawer from a storage unit.

He was watching her, all right.

"Stop checking out my ass, von Kreus," she said without looking up.

"Can't help myself," he confessed, and figured now was as good a time as any to make his move. He strolled up behind her so when she straightened, his front brushed her backside. "It's such a nice one," he murmured in her ear.

She jumped and whirled. If he hadn't reached out and caught her around the waist, she would have fallen backward. It was just the gentlemanly thing to do.

Kissing her wasn't exactly gentlemanly, but he couldn't help himself on that one, either. She'd been driving him crazy for the past three days, keeping him at arm's length. She'd gone out to dinner with him each night because he insisted, but she'd carefully avoided touching him again. She was a big tease and he wanted another taste of her.

He plunged his hand into her hair and held her still while she hung on to the drawer. He thrust his tongue between her lips. She gasped, making it easy on him. He leaned in.

He felt a distinct shiver sift through her body before she tore her mouth from his. He released her and stepped back. Better not to push his luck.

"That was nice," he said, moving aside so she could stomp past him. *"Liefde."*

At the vault door, she ran smack into Claude. Who grinned and let her pass. When she was gone, he turned to Witt. "My brother," Claude said, "would you be interested in a little job on the side?"

Witt's pulse sped. This was so much sooner than he'd ever dared hope. "What kind of job?"

"Something right up your alley."

"Yeah? Like what?"

"We have captured one of our enemies. We'd like you to interrogate him."

Chapter 3

The man was annoying as hell. But good, Marina had to admit…if grudgingly. Three days it had taken Witt to get next to the bad guys. She'd been working at Glace Chaud over two weeks and hadn't even gotten close.

She was not too surprised it was the doorman, Claude, and not Monsieur Henri who'd made the overture to Witt. She'd never felt the store manager was part of the illegal diamond operation, other than supplying a sales venue. He was slimy enough to sell cheap contraband diamonds, but didn't seem smart enough or brave enough to be part of the real dirty work.

Witt told her about Claude's proposition at

dinner after work. It had become a habit, him asking her to dinner, her saying no, him hauling her along like a caveman anyway, trying all evening to charm her into having sex with him, until she slammed her door in his face and went to bed alone. The truth? Wishing like hell she'd dared let him join her. Hell, even cavemen had their charms.

"Claude wants you to interrogate someone?" she asked.

"His boss does."

"Camara?"

"That would be my guess. Maybe whoever it is will show up to watch me question the guy. Then we'll know for sure."

"Why would they trust you, a stranger, with something like this?"

His eyebrows flicked. "I'm good at making strangers trust me."

She nodded. It had certainly worked on her.

"Interrogation is my specialty, Marina."

She knew Witt was South African, but not much else about him. Her section chief at SIS, James Dalgliesh, wouldn't release Witt's file to her. "Sorry, it's on a need-to-know basis only," Dalgliesh had said.

"If I have to work with the guy, I should know about him," she'd objected.

"I'm not making the decisions on this one. Orders came from above. Way above. Like Downing Street above."

The Prime Minister? Good Lord. That kind of

clout had to have someone bigger behind it than Witt. Yeah, like Corbett Lazlo.

But Corbett had been equally close-mouthed when she'd called him. "I'd rather Witt tell you himself what he wants you to know," Corbett had said, to her supreme annoyance.

Which, of course, had made her even more suspicious. Hello? Her job? So she'd resorted to doing some research online. She wasn't sure what she'd expected from the results, but somehow she'd envisioned a vastly different scenario for DeWitt von Kreus than what had turned up on the search engine.

Though, God knew if any of it was real or was simply misinformation put there by the Lazlo Group.

"You're an interrogator?" she asked him now, thinking it was the perfect opportunity to find out more. "For the Lazlo Group?"

"Information retrieval specialist. And for a long time before that. Before working for Corbett, I was an interrogator for the African National Congress military branch, before the end of apartheid."

She blinked. So it was true. "Really? The ANC. That's Nelson Mandela's organization, right?"

"Well, there's more to it than just one man, but, yes. Basically."

"But you're white," she prodded. "Afrikaans, if I'm not mistaken."

His brow arched. "And your point is?"

Okay. Bad subject. She cleared her throat. "Nothing. Just unusual, that's all."

He sighed, as if he'd had to explain this many

times in the past. "I realize that a few of my more conservative countrymen have a reputation for being…backward thinking. I'm not. I hate injustice. Of any kind. It's why I did what I did. It's why I still do what I do. Call me an idealist, but in my vision of the world, the color of your skin doesn't matter and good wins over evil."

She nodded. The guy had just gone up about two million points in her book. If she were keeping score. Which she wasn't.

"I respect that," she said. More than he knew. "So, when do we meet with Claude?"

His gaze shot to hers, along with a frown. "Not we. Me."

She smiled. "You horned in on *my* grid, von Kreus. You're stuck with me, whether you like it or not."

He leaned back in his chair. Tonight they were eating in a small bistro off the Trocadero. White linen tablecloths, dark wooden chairs and a long bar with sparkling glasses hanging above it made it inviting and typically French. Busy waiters hurried to and fro. The food was great and the place was already crowded, even though it was still early for dinner by continental standards.

She ordered two cups of coffee from a passing waiter—they'd eaten together often enough now that she didn't have to ask—and when the waiter left, Witt leaned forward, hands folded on the white linen where his plate had been. *Oh, boy, here it comes.* The "Too dangerous for the little lady" speech.

"These are dangerous men, Marina. Suspicious men. If they even think we're not who we say we are, we are dead. Let me handle this on my own. Please."

She sighed. Just once, she'd like to be wrong. "What part of 'I do this for a living' don't you get?"

His hands gripped each other like he was restraining them from throttling her. "You don't understand."

What was there to understand? Unless... An unpleasant thought came to her. One she'd had before. "What's the matter von Kreus? Afraid for me to see you in action? Perhaps you use torture? Is that it?"

He snapped back as though she'd slapped him. "I've never tortured a human being in my life, and I don't aim to start now," he growled.

"Then why the price on your head?"

His blue eyes narrowed and went hot. "I see you've been doing your homework."

"Just like to know who I'm dealing with."

"Then why hasn't this come up before now?"

"I was hoping you'd volunteer the information on your own."

A corner of his mouth curled up cynically, his mustache striking a deceptively rakish pose. "I'm not much for pillow talk. Especially when there's no pillow involved."

Nice try, mate. "Are you saying if I'd shared my bed with you, you'd have shared your secrets with me?"

He gave a short, wry laugh. "Maybe. It's a matter of trust, Marina. If you don't even trust me with your body, how can you possibly think I'd trust you with information that could get me killed?"

He had a point there. "The thinking's warped, but I guess I get it." She forced a smile and thanked the waiter when he came with their coffees. "And by the way," she said after he'd gone, "it's not that I don't trust you with my body. I do. I mean, I would, if—" She shook her head to banish an image of just how far she'd trusted him already. "Look, I just don't think it's a good idea for us to get involved."

He leaned forward and took her hand. "Who said anything about getting involved? It's just sex, *liefde*. Nothing complicated."

Maybe not for him. She sighed, and reluctantly allowed herself a moment of weakness. She didn't pull her hand from his. It felt…good…holding hers. Warm. Strong. Capable. "Sex is always complicated, Witt," she said. "Especially in our business."

He lifted her fingers to his lips and pressed a kiss to them. "Believe me, it doesn't have to be." He turned his wrist to check his watch. His whole demeanor changed. "Speaking of business, I better get going."

She felt oddly deflated at his sudden change. Immediately she removed her hand from his, appalled with herself. Had she really wanted him to talk her into sleeping with him? Good Lord. What was it about the man that made all her good sense fly right out the window? Getting involved with him would be such a bad idea. And yet she found herself constantly battling the impulse to break down and surrender to his not-so-subtle seduction.

"I told you, I'm coming with you," she said,

forcing herself back on task. "But I'll need to stop at my place to change first."

He regarded her for a long moment. No doubt weighing how to talk her out of going along.

"If you don't take me, I'll just follow you," she told him, putting any discussion at an end. "And I'll send you the bill if my suit gets messed up because you wouldn't let me change. It's a Chanel."

He made one of those impatient male noises halfway between a huff and a tsk. "Now who's being obnoxious?"

She batted her eyelashes. "*My* specialty."

"God help me," he muttered in defeat, and led the way out of the bistro. After a few minutes of broody silence, he said, "So tell me, how good are you at playing bad cop?"

She chuckled. "Take a wild guess."

"Why is it I have no trouble believing that?" he said pointedly, slinging his arm around her shoulders as they walked to the car.

His question surprised her. Most of her male peers at SIS—make that *all* her male peers—made her play the good cop. Men always thought they were so much tougher than women, and constantly felt they had to prove it.

But what surprised her even more was how difficult she was finding it to step away from Witt's touches. More so each time he casually put his arm around her, or his hand to the small of her back, or even stole a kiss. Which had been often after that first one this morning. Witt had touched her more in just a few hours than some men had during months of dating. Of course, most men tended to be guarded around a woman carrying a gun. On their best behavior. Which was one of the reasons she'd stopped dating. What was the point? Civilian men were scared of her…and she was scared of getting close to a man in her own profession who could be dead tomorrow.

Wow. Where had that come from?

From her mother. That's where. Her mother had been quietly terrified every day of her short but intense marriage to Marina's US Secret Service agent father. Her parents had split up when she was seven—just after the harrowing incident in which Corbett Lazlo had saved Marina's life. That had been the last straw for her gun-shy British mother. After the divorce, Marina had lived with her mother in England until she had gone back to the States to attend Georgetown University in DC. There she'd gotten reacquainted with her dad, and both realized to their amazement that she was far more suited to Dad's fast-paced, dangerous lifestyle than the peaceful life on Mother's tranquil country estate. Make that *boring* country estate….

"*Skatie?* You there?"

Marina snapped back to the present with a start. By the look on his face, Witt must have been trying to get her attention. She blinked. And discovered her backside was leaning against Witt's silver Land Rover, and his front was leaning against her. Intimately. His hands gripped the roof to either side of her, bracketing her in. Her own hands had somehow landed on his hips. Okay, fine, his butt.

Bollox.

She yanked them off him, crossing her arms over her abdomen. "What?"

He had the audacity to look amused. "Like I was saying, I think we should practice."

"Practice what?" As soon as the words left her mouth she knew she'd made a mistake.

"Good cop, bad cop."

"Ah." Trying desperately to ignore his cocky grin and stick to business, she tried a diversionary tactic. "Why do you want me to be the bad cop?"

"Part of my interrogation technique. I'm always the good guy." He leaned in closer, undiverted. "Besides, you know I've been wanting you to let loose your bad side, Marina."

You had to give the guy credit for persistence. She pushed him back. Or attempted to. He didn't budge a centimeter. "I think you're mixing up bad cop with bad girl, von Kreus."

He shifted closer still, moving his boots to either side of her high heels, capturing her legs between his. The stiff wool of his trousers pressed into her bare calves and ankles. It was an incredibly sexual posture, dominant, and assertive of a kind of male claim that should have made her furious. Instead it felt...*oh, God*...thrilling. He was a handsome, powerful, dangerous man. And he wanted her. Enough to pressure her. Enough to tempt her into surrender.

Not that it would take much.

"If you're going with me tonight to meet Claude and his contacts, you're coming as my woman, my fiancée. My partner in crime *and* in bed. We have to be convincing. You can't have any missish hesitancy over kissing me or touching me, or it won't work. They won't buy it unless it's real."

She swallowed. And knew he was right. It was infuriating, but because of his maneuvering her into pretending to be engaged, she now had to choose. Stay out of it, or get over her reluctance to let him close. Regardless of the consequences to her body. To her heart.

Slowly she raised her hands to his chest. He was wearing another one of those expensive suits with a silk shirt and tie. The fabric felt smooth and warm beneath her fingers and against her legs. Warmed by the heat of his body. A body that rippled with strength and pulsed with sexual energy.

If a woman was going to surrender, this was definitely the kind of body she should lose herself to.

Over the smells of the street and the passing cars, Witt's unique male scent spilled over her, beckoning her to give in. It compelled her to slide her arms under his jacket, to put her nose to his silky collar and breathe deeply of it. Of him. He smelled dark and musky, enticing; like hot, lazy sex on cool, rumpled sheets.

She lifted her face and kissed him. He didn't help at all. He stood solid and unmoving, the Rock of Gibraltar, as she slowly brushed her lips back and forth over his, flicking them with her tongue, tickling her nose on his sexy mustache, so she was awash with the erotic taste of him, drowning in the arousing smell and feel of him.

Someone moaned.

He pulled away, gripping her shoulders with firm hands. Or was there a fine tremble in them? "Okay. I think you've got the idea. We better move before—" He didn't complete the sentence, just gave his head a shake and jerked open the car door for her.

There was no hiding his arousal. When she slid into the Rover's front seat, it was right at eye level. Rampant. Hungry.

Against her better judgment she darted her gaze up and met his. The look he returned made her shiver clear to her toes. Not from the cold. But from the heat in his eyes.

And that's when she knew she was in trouble.

Big, dangerous, blue-eyed trouble.

The guy they wanted Witt to interrogate was a flunky gofer for a rival diamond dealer. Young, maybe seventeen or so, scrawny with stringy brown hair and track marks on his arms. French. Scared spitless.

Witt almost sighed. This would be so easy it was almost insulting.

So he decided to shift his focus to learning as much as he could from Claude and the two tough compatriots he'd introduced as Mfana and Deco.

They'd driven two cars deep into the *banlieux*— the rundown suburban projects on the fringes of Paris. The place was rough. Very rough. He worried about the Land Rover when he parked it in the half-deserted lot and opened the door for Marina. So he paid an urchin, whom Claude summoned from a dirty stoop, to keep an eye on it. Double the going rate. Good thing he'd brought lots of cash. Before leaving he made sure the kid saw his gun.

The elevator in the building Claude had brought them to had long since ceased to function, so after a six-story climb, picking their way through layers of garbage, junkies and their discarded paraphernalia, Witt, Marina and the three Africans trooped into a rat hole of a two-room flat that had obviously lacked paying occupants for a long time. Kitchen cabinet doors hung askew. Grime covered the few windows, lending a puke-brown tinge to the feeble moonlight that managed to filter through them. The whole place smelled like rats and urine. *Lekker.* Very nice.

There was no furniture other than one wobbly wooden chair, to which the young French gofer had been duct-taped. How long had he been sitting there? Hours? Days?

Mfana hung back to guard the door. Deco walked over and leaned against a dirty wall behind the prisoner, checking his fingernails as though bored. The French kid stared at Witt, wild-eyed from above the duct tape sealing his mouth shut, jerking at his bound wrists and ankles, which made the chair rock so violently it was in danger of falling over.

Witt stared back at the kid for a moment, then turned to Claude. "Are you serious? This boy can't possibly know anything worth even the effort of climbing those stairs."

Claude shrugged. "I agree. But my boss wants to be sure."

"Your boss must be an idiot. Perhaps I should talk to him myself."

Claude just showed his big white teeth. All right, so Witt would have to prove himself first.

"Who cares?" Marina cut in, in a brash, nasal voice Witt had never heard from her before. Her bad-cop voice? "We're here now. Let's start the fun."

All eyes turned to her. Well, some of them had already been on her. Mfana and Deco were far more interested in what *she* was doing than in Witt or the prisoner. Who could blame them? Claude had been more than surprised when Marina was with him at the pick-up. Especially in the outfit she was wearing.

At her flat she'd shocked Witt by changing into a deliciously short leather skirt and mouthwateringly tight T-shirt with the sleeves and collar—a *lot* of the collar—cut raggedly out of it. BITCH was spelled out in rhinestones across the swell of her far-too-exposed breasts. Both pink. Her skirt and T-shirt, not her breasts. Although—

Verdomme. Damn! Not going there. Not now.

Witt had explained to Claude that they worked as a team. The other man had looked skeptical, but conceded without comment. Witt and Marina both had to prove themselves. But his body was still clenched and his brain set to short-circuit at the least provocation because of their little curbside *graunch* session earlier. He must have been insane to let her kiss him like that, right before conducting business.

He'd barely resisted throwing her in the Land Rover and taking her then.

Maybe she was right. Sex was too distracting.

And now…*yessus,* seeing her long legs and perfect ass bending over in that sex-kitten pink skirt was sending his hormones into another freefall of lust. God help him. He had to have her soon or lose it completely.

Concentrate, von Kreus. Concentrate!

She was leaning over the tied-up kid, peering into his panicked eyes. "This'll teach you not to listen to your mommy," she sing-songed. The words were softly spoken but they sent a shiver up even Witt's spine.

In her flat she'd chilled him to the bone when she'd produced a small collection of very nasty and very sharp implements. "I got these off a terrorist I arrested," she'd explained. "Thought they might come in handy someday." Today must be the day. Lucky kid.

Damn, she was good at this bad-cop thing. Very good. Of course, it was easy to be evil when someone was there to back you off when things were about to go over the edge. He'd never had that luxury. Which was why he always played the good guy. Threatening things you weren't willing to do usually got you into trouble.

He glanced at the kid who was watching Marina, looking less scared but more clueless. It must be the pink outfit. You didn't expect a woman in pink to be a monster. The kid should have taken a clue from the word in rhinestones.

"Maybe you should let me try first, *skat,*" Witt offered.

She slid her shoulder bag off, opened it and started to pull the implements out, handing them to him as she did. "Why bother? You heard. The man with our paycheck wants him to tell us everything he knows. That means I'm up."

The kid's eyes widened to saucers when it finally registered what was coming out of her bag. Knives. Razor blades. Coldly lethal surgical instruments. A battery-operated device with bare wires sticking out of it. The kid abruptly started screaming under the duct tape.

Witt had seen worse. God, so much worse. Both the instruments and the results. But to a young boy, no matter how streetwise, who'd never experienced the horrors of war, the array had to be impressive. Witt almost felt sorry for him. Almost. But then he reminded himself the kid willingly worked for a terrorist who routinely killed innocent African people, including kids younger than this one, in the name of greed.

Witt handed off the torture instruments to Claude, then slid his arms around Marina's waist from behind. "*Eish,* babe, he's just a pup. Let me have a go at him, hey? Be a shame to spoil his good looks. Permanently, anyway."

Marina snorted. "You goin' soft on me, stud?"

He chuckled in her ear. "Never." He even let her feel how true that was.

He didn't miss her surprised intake of breath,

though she stifled it quickly. But it stalled audibly in her lungs when he deliberately let his hand wander up to caress her breast. The nipple sprang to attention under his palm. But there was also a sudden tenseness in her muscles; he could feel her urge to wrench herself away from him and run for the door.

Too bad. She'd chosen to come with him, as his fiancée. She'd known the rules. He might be playing the good cop, but he was in charge here. At least of her.

She surprised him by turning in his arms and twining her own about his neck. She gave him a long, thorough kiss. "Come on, let me at him. Pretty please?" She said it with a sexy pout.

Every eye in the room was on her. Excited. Anticipating. They were all buying her act. Hell, *he* was buying it.

It was a dangerous game to be playing without rehearsal. But so far it was going well. It felt natural to be working with her. Like they were perfectly in sync.

He puffed out a breath, as though deciding his answer. Then he nodded, and tilted his head at Claude to give her back the hardware. Claude did so, his smile wide, and said, "I see what you mean by seeing her in action, my brother. You are not what I expected, *mademoiselle*."

Marina snickered as she considered the knives in her hand. "I'm usually not." One of her biggest assets as an agent. No one expected the Spanish Inquisition from a pretty blonde in Chanel. Or a pink miniskirt.

The boy's tape-muffled cries got more frantic as she

selected a particularly ugly blade from the bunch and held it up for his inspection. The kid pissed his pants. His eyes darted to Witt in wild supplication, rocking the chair forward, trying to jump it toward him.

Again Witt felt a tug of sympathy. The kid was damn lucky to be dealing with him and Marina, but he couldn't know that. Hopefully this experience would scare him straight.

"You got something to say, kid?" he asked, casually putting his fingers around the back of Marina's neck and rubbing slow circles on her skin. A subtle claim of authority, but unmistakable to anyone watching. He kissed her temple lingeringly before he finally glanced toward the kid, who was nodding madly, as though his life depended on it. Which it probably did. Claude and the gang didn't look like they fooled around. A crude beating, cigarette burns and a bullet to the head were more their speed.

Witt ripped the duct tape from the boy's mouth as quickly as he could. The kid didn't make a squeak until it was all off, and Witt looked at his watch and said, "Talk. You've got thirty seconds."

Then you couldn't shut him up. In less than a minute, they knew who the leader of the rival outfit was, the key French and African players, when the last shipment of rough diamonds had arrived from the Congo and how they'd been slipped through customs, as well as who'd polished up the stones for resale to the European dealers. Oh, yeah, and when the next shipment of diamonds was due.

Not a bad sixty seconds of work. And maybe Claude's boss wasn't so stupid after all. Who'd have thought this weasly kid would be trusted with so much information? Didn't say much for the rival that a gofer would have been allowed to hear all this. Or maybe the kid was higher up than Claude believed.

Deco pulled a gun out of his waistband and pointed it at the kid's head. "Wait," Witt said, holding out a hand. "Some of the names he gave were only first names. You need him alive to point out faces on the street."

Claude waved the gun away. "He's right. The boss wants all of his rivals taken out. Every last one. We make a mistake and it's our hides."

"What's your name, kid?" Witt asked. "Where do you live?"

"Etienne." The boy was trembling so hard his teeth chattered as he gave his address. "It's my mother's house. She has nothing to do with this. Please don't hurt her."

From the corner of his eye, he saw Marina's jaw tighten.

"Then you better do as you're told," Witt told him. He gripped the kid's hair and jerked his face up for emphasis. The kid nodded vigorously. Witt pointed at Claude. "You are working for this man now." More vigorous agreement. After drilling the kid a look that made him whimper in fear, Witt cut the rest of Etienne's bonds. "Get out of here," he growled. "And don't forget, we know where your mama lives."

At least for another hour or two. As soon as they were away from this place he'd call Corbett and have her moved.

The kid ran out of the flat like a shot.

Watching him flee, Deco said angrily to Claude, "The woman's right. Your friend is soft. We should have killed the little snitch. He will betray us."

"No," Claude said. "Witt handled it well. We got all the information we needed, and now we also have a hostage if we need one. He won't dare betray us. Later, if the boss wants him dead, now where to find him."

"You really think he'll stick around?" Deco said with a sneer.

Claude looked complacent. "Yes. If he wants to live." He clapped Witt on the back. "Excellent work, my brother. The boss will be pleased."

"My pleasure. Tell your boss I'm available whenever he needs me."

"Don't you mean *us,* sweetheart?" Marina sauntered up and slipped her arms around him. "We work as a team," she repeated to Claude. "Wherever he goes, I go."

"Which right now means my place," Witt said, leaning down to swoop her into a kiss. "Because I'm going home and having an early night of it. Been a long week."

"Mmmm," she said, kissing him back. "Sounds good."

He knew she was just playacting for the benefit of their audience. He wasn't. Before the night was out, he intended to have her in his flat and in his bed. Naked and sighing his name. Or maybe screaming it. Beaut. Screaming was good.

She must have sensed what he was thinking. Or seen it in his eyes. Because she pulled away and half an hour later when they'd finally taken leave of Claude and his duo of cutthroats, trotted down the six flights of filthy stairs and out to the Land Rover—which was thankfully intact—and paid the urchin watching it, she'd barely buckled into the passenger seat before saying, "Just drop me at the nearest Métro station. I'll take the train home."

He almost smiled. She really thought she could resist him. But she couldn't. No more than the kid had. True, she'd played a big part in that success, but she would in this one, too. Her own desire for him would be her downfall. Just as the kid's fear had been his.

"Splitting up wouldn't be very smart," Witt said with a completely neutral expression as he grabbed his mobile phone and punched the speed dial. "You told them you were spending the night with me. That Deco character doesn't trust us one bit as it is. I'm betting he tails us."

Deco, bless his mistrustful heart, in fact did just that. In his bright-red classic Chevy Nova. All the way to Witt's place, while Witt filled Corbett in on the events of the evening and Marina seethed. The Nova stayed several car lengths back trying to remain unobtrusive, but it was just too painfully noticeable.

She wasn't happy, but she was trapped.

She had to go with him. She had to walk straight into his house. Straight into his hands.

And if he had anything to say about it, straight into his bed.

Chapter 4

*D*amn *my big mouth.*

Marina pressed her back against the closed entry
door to Witt's flat, knowing she had no choice but to
be there, but not liking it one damned bit. He had
walked inside before her and thrown his suit coat on
the sofa, drawn his SIG from its shoulder holster
and headed into the depths of the apartment. He
hadn't looked alarmed; probably just his usual
coming-home routine.

"Lock the door," he'd called, then disappeared
down a hall.

He was being casual about her presence, almost
to the point of ignoring her.

But she wasn't falling for the act.

He was just as acutely aware of her being on his turf—she almost wanted to say in his lair—as she was. She could smell it in the air—his awareness and hers. There was a hum of sexual anticipation, a push of sexual energy in the room thick as fog. Like lightning gathering to strike. Already her body was reacting to it—tightening, quickening, drenching.

She glanced around in desperation, seeking a way out of her untenable situation. She homed in on the large picture window overlooking the rooftops of Paris and went over to it. Maybe Deco had left. Down on the street, six floors below, the bright-red Nova was still parked at the curb. Her hope deflated.

She turned, examining the room, searching for a plausible method of escape. She was in a large living-dining room combination, all done in sleek, low Scandinavian furniture and painted in muted beiges and browns. Bright splashes of color from a collection of African masks and native carvings punctuated the walls and shelves. A large sisal rug covered the floor above thick Berber carpeting. It was a very masculine room. Thank God there were no animal heads. Marina herself would be trophy enough. She didn't want to share the space with his other conquests.

Not that she had any plans to break down. She was just a realist.

"Make yourself comfortable. Drink?" Witt asked, strolling into the room and pulling off his tie. The gun and holster were gone. His feet were bare.

He tossed the tie onto the sofa next to his jacket

and headed for a drinks cabinet set into the built-in shelves. When he lifted the lid it lit up inside, shedding a pretty glow over the surrounding books and objets d'art. She'd love to see it up close, if she dared move. Which she didn't.

"What would you like?" he asked.

She answered honestly. "To get out of here."

He turned and smiled, a solid brown bottle in his hand. "You scared of me again, *skat?*"

"You bet."

"And yet you're the one carrying a gun."

"I'm not worried about you shooting me, Witt."

To his credit he didn't make the obvious come-back. Just smiled wider and poured a clear liquid into two small crystal glasses. He walked over, took her purse from her and sent it sailing to join the other things on the sofa, then handed her one of the glasses.

"You'll feel more relaxed after a shot."

"I doubt it."

He laughed. "You're sweet." It was disconcerting how not worried he appeared. Did he think she'd be that easy?

Unfortunately, he was probably right. The man was sexy as the devil, and she wanted him more than she'd ever wanted a man before in her life. At the moment she was having a hard time remembering why this was such a bad idea.

He clicked his glass to hers, raised it and waited for her to do the same. His expression was amused, indulgent, patient. His eyes twinkled, blue as a clear morning sky. There were little smile crinkles at the corners. And worry lines around his smiling mouth. The face of a man who lived hard. And loved harder.

So tempting...

What was *wrong* with her? She'd always been able to control her hormones before around inappropriate men. *That* was why it was a bad idea. Her lack of control around him. Always a situation to be avoided.

With a sinking feeling, she clicked his glass, and they threw back their shots. And she thought...perhaps it was the fact that he *wasn't* inappropriate that was making her so confused. Hell, if she wanted a bout of hot, uncomplicated sex, this man couldn't be more appropriate. Smart, handsome, civilized and he had top-secret clearance. What more could a girl ask for?

Right. And that was the *real* problem. The smart, handsome and civilized part.

If she slept with him, she'd fall for him. There was no doubt in her mind. She already had a seriously wicked crush on the man after knowing him all of three days. He'd gotten to her, penetrated her defenses to a depth no other man had ever been able to reach. If she gave him her body again, she may as well kiss her heart goodbye.

He took her empty glass and set it down on the marble-topped coffee table along with his own, then put his arm around her and guided her over to the long, low sofa.

"Sit," he said, and because she'd look awful silly standing up all night, she did. He sat down right next to her, the side of his body pressed intimately to hers. It was a comfortable sofa with a broad seat and slanting back, designed to encourage a relaxed sprawl. She slid down and rested her head on top of the back cushion. Attempting nonchalance in her pink miniskirt. Yeah, right.

"Now," he said, stretching out his long, muscular legs and crossing his bare ankles. He slid a shade closer to her. "What are you so worried about?"

She snorted softly but didn't answer. More like what *wasn't* she worried about?

He took her hand and held it between his. "Marina, you have a unique opportunity here. A man who actually listens. Talk to me."

She sighed and rolled her head to look at him. "So you can cajole me out of my objections?"

His smile was unrepentant. "Maybe." He tipped his head. "Unless you'd rather I forget all that and just start kissing you instead?"

She felt her eyes widen. But something…unintended…must have shown on her face because he said, "Ah," and suddenly his mouth was covering hers.

She tried to pull away. Really she did. But it was too late. She was already drowning in him. In the taste of him. In the texture and pliancy of his tongue as it swept over hers. In the feel of being enveloped by his strong, insistent arms. In the longing she felt for him in her whole being.

He kissed her deeply, thoroughly, for long, endless minutes—hours?—of bliss. He kissed her and kissed her and kissed her until she was lost in the drugging spell of his tongue and his lips, and felt dizzy with want for the rest of him. She moaned, and whispered, "Witt."

He pulled back a fraction, looking as disoriented as she felt. He put his forehead to hers, kissing her cheeks and nose and eyes as they both fought to catch their breath. He didn't push her prone on the sofa, didn't try to peel off her clothes. Though at this point she wouldn't have stopped him. Her body throbbed, a hot, aching mass of unfulfilled need. Damn, she *was* that easy.

"Marina, please," he murmured between breaths. "I want you. I want to take your beautiful body and make it mine. All mine."

He paused, as though waiting for her to respond. To give him permission. She wanted to agree; she did. She wanted to tell him yes, take me. But even with the erotic taste of him spicing her tongue with desire, it wouldn't cooperate. She couldn't. Something deep inside her made her hold back. Yes, she would surrender. But she couldn't give. Not—

"I won't hurt you, I swear," he whispered.

She stroked her fingers through his thick mane of hair. It was long and blond like an African lion's, streaked by the outdoor sun, carrying the scent of him, musky and masculine. She touched the matching mustache, warm and moist from her own kisses.

A thick coil of wanting twisted through her body, like a living thing. "I know you won't."

"Then what are you afraid of, Marina? Tell me."

She trembled in his arms, suddenly freezing. How to explain something she wasn't sure she understood herself?

She was silent for a long time. Longer than most men would have waited for an answer. But Witt wasn't most men. He held her close and waited patiently, rubbing his hand up and down her back in a soothing motion.

Finally she shuddered out a breath. "I understand where you're coming from, Witt. In our business you tend to grab happiness and pleasure where and when you can. I get that. I've done it. We've all done it. That's what happened in that hotel room the first time we met."

He gave her temple a lingering kiss. Didn't agree. Didn't disagree. Didn't say a word.

"But I don't do it very often," she continued. "I'm not really into casual sex."

He brushed a strand of hair back from her face. "So I gathered."

She pulled back and gazed into his clear blue eyes. He didn't look like a man bent on seduction. He looked like a man bent on…understanding. Her heart squeezed. This would be so much easier if he were just a one-track-minded skirt chaser.

"The thing is, *liefde,* I'm not offering you casual sex. Believe me, I know we can't become involved, really involved. I am certainly not in a position to offer you a romantic relationship in the traditional sense. I am most definitely not looking for any kind of commitment from you. And I know you feel the same way. "But—" he gave a heartfelt sigh "—I'd like a woman I can come to and feel safe with. A woman who will share her company and her body, in what little time we might have together. A woman I can be myself with."

His eyes looked so serious as he spoke. Not a hint of deception or agenda. It was an incredibly seductive offer. Far more seductive than even his kisses and hard body.

How she longed to accept!

She forced a shake of her head. "It'll get too messy. I don't think I can separate physical closeness from all those other kinds of feelings. You'll feel awkward. And I'll get hurt." She shook her head. "Trust me, it can't work."

"You mean you're afraid you'll fall in love with me?"

She glanced away. This was not a conversation she wanted to have. There was such a thing as too much honesty. But he looked so earnest. "Maybe," she admitted. "In the worst case."

He smiled at her then, the hot African sun shining in his eyes. "I'm not afraid of a woman's love, Marina. And you won't be hurt as long as you understand from the beginning that, for me, it can't be about more than sex and friendship."

She blinked, wondering how to react to that revealing bit of oh-so-male naiveté.

"I'm not looking for a wife," he said, almost sadly. "I will never marry. You, or anyone else."

"Why not?" she asked, surprised by his brutal

honesty. Then gasped at what he was probably thinking. "No, I mean—"

"It's okay. You have every right to ask."

She squirmed, uncomfortable with the level of personal revelation the conversation had reached. "No, really. I don't want to know."

"It's because of my past. What I've done. What I've seen. My parents are happily married. They've been madly in love for over forty years. They know every last thing about each other. No secrets. All of those things bring them closer together. But with me…" He let out a humorless laugh. "It would drive a woman screaming into the night to know all my secrets."

A depth of pain such as she'd seldom before witnessed shadowed his eyes. "Oh, Witt," she whispered.

But as quickly as that, the shadow was gone. He gave her a wry, sexy smile, filled with self-deprecation and a gathering swell of heat. "So go on and fall in love with me, Marina Bond. I'll make it worth your while, hey?" He leaned in and played his tongue across her lips. "Just don't ask me my secrets. And don't ask for more than my body. But that I will gladly give you, for as long as you want it."

She let out a breath. Suddenly she was more confused than ever. It wasn't that she wanted a man, or to marry, or any of the things he was implying. No way. She didn't want a commitment any more than he did. But…could she give herself to a man—to Witt—and possibly let herself fall in love with him, and not expect more? She had never even considered the possibility. She was unprepared to decide. Had no way of assessing the consequences of a course of action so unlike her.

What had he said? A woman he could feel safe with, be himself with? He made it sound so…appealing. Exactly like what she needed, too. With none of the usual hazards. But…

He must have sensed the crack in her armor. Before she knew what he was doing, he slid down onto his back on the sofa and toppled her on top of his chest. He used his toes to scrape off her high heels and kick them to the floor.

"Witt, what are you doing?"

"Helping you make up your mind."

He tugged her down and slipped his hands under her T-shirt, then cupped her breasts, flicking her nipples with his thumbs. She squirmed, moaning softly in pleasure.

How did he always know exactly what to do to make her want to beg him for more?

"No need to beg, *liefde*," he whispered.

Surely, she hadn't said that aloud?

He unfastened her bra and pulled it and her T-shirt off, exposing her breasts completely. He brought her closer, taking her aching flesh into his mouth, using his teeth and his very clever tongue to drive her mad with want. She let her body melt into his, all the way down. This time it was Witt who moaned. She was sure it was him. Her legs straddled his hips, catching his arousal in the juncture of her thighs.

He laved and sucked. She writhed and ground. They both panted and moaned.

And suddenly she was on her back and he was on top.

He gazed down at her with half-lidded eyes spilling over with desire. *For her.* He leaned down and whispered in her ear. Told her what he intended do to her. Sensual things. Erotic things. Things that made her blush with embarrassment. Things that made her wet with anticipation.

She closed her eyes and let his low, gravelly voice stroke over her body like callused fingers. Or maybe it really was his fingers. *Yes, it was.* They touched her, driving her need higher, ridding her of her skirt and panties, coaxing her to open to him, urging her to surrender.

She was already naked. Already trembling with need. She could surrender.

"Marina," he ordered softly. "Open your eyes."

She was naked, but she suddenly became aware that he was still fully dressed. Heat ripped across her face. Her vulnerable position under him was driven home by the contrast of her pale skin to his black trousers and white shirt.

His body was big, so much bigger than hers. So powerful. Dominant. He lay above her, pinning her to the sofa with fourteen stone of solid muscle. She wasn't going anywhere unless he allowed it.

A shiver trilled down her spine. It should have been from fear. It wasn't.

"Take off your clothes," she whispered.

He whisked his shirt over his head, then held himself above her as though doing push-ups. "Are you sure about this?"

She nodded. "Yes," she whispered.

His gaze swept down the length of her body, like a predator trying to decide what morsel of his prey to eat first.

She changed her mind. "No, I'm not!"

A corner of his mouth curved up. "Don't worry. I'm sure enough for both of us."

"You would be," she said, panicking, trying to wriggle free.

He didn't let her. The other corner curved up. "How about if I convince you?"

She stilled. She licked her lips, and his eyes followed the movement hungrily. He levered down and captured her mouth with his. His broad, bare chest brushed her breasts, tickling them with his coarse chest hair. His arousal felt long and thick between her thighs. She arched up, wrapping her legs around him and her arms about his neck.

Her pulse thrummed. She loved the way he felt lying on top of her. Loved the weight of his body pressing into hers. Loved the brush of his corded muscles and wiry hair against her sensitive skin. Loved the hard length of him straining to breach the barriers between them and fill her.

She knew she'd regret doing this. Knew it as surely as she knew her own name.

But she'd regret it more if she didn't.

Just one night. Was that too much to ask? Just one

night, before she went back to her lonely, solitary existence. One night of being with a man who rocked her world to the core.

Tomorrow she could worry about consequences. Tomorrow she would think about the future. About her heart. Tonight she wanted to be his.

Tonight she wanted to forget her own name.

Witt had never experienced lovemaking this intense.

In fact, he wasn't sure he'd ever really made love before tonight with Marina.

Marina.

She was so beautiful. So vulnerable. So responsive to his affection. So everything he wanted in a woman. So everything he should stay a thousand klicks away from.

But he hadn't been able to help himself. He wanted her that badly. And he'd be damned if he'd let himself develop a conscience about taking what was offered. Not that he intended to hurt her. Never on purpose. But she'd called it. He would probably hurt her anyway. Because of who he was. What he was. A man like Witt von Kreus wasn't worthy of a woman like Marina Bond.

But that wouldn't stop him. Not tonight. Maybe tomorrow he'd be able to backpedal and tell her she'd been right and they'd made a huge mistake.

Maybe.

But not tonight. Not with her sweet, soft body tucked under his, open for his taking. Not with her moaning his name, screaming his name, sighing his name. Not on his life.

He brought her to climax twice on the sofa before carrying her to his bed, where he plunged into her deep and hard, pumping her over the edge a third time. He could still feel her nails on his back, the sweet pleasure-pain of her passion.

Yerre, she turned him on. He couldn't get enough of her. He wanted to bury himself in her and not pull out until he'd made her hoarse from screaming, until they were both breathless, boneless puddles of quivering, sated flesh, unable to tell her body from his. Until he'd claimed her so compellingly and so thoroughly she'd never want to be with another man, ever again.

So he did. And when the first light of dawn was creeping over the windowsill, he held her in his arms and sighed with contentment.

So this was what his parents experienced every morning of their marriage. How amazing! No wonder they were still so much in love with each other.

For the first time ever, Witt felt a glimmer of regret over the decision he'd made all those years ago never to marry. A brief, poignant stab of sorrow that he would never experience those same things with a woman. *With this woman.*

He kissed her lips and closed his eyes and told himself he was being a sentimental fool. As he started to drift off, he prayed he'd wake in the morning as his old self.

Remember Sarah, he told himself.

No regrets. No ties. No promises. No pain.

That was him. That was who he had to be. No choice.

To think otherwise was a delusion he couldn't afford to indulge. To wish otherwise was simply inviting another heartache. And heartache was something he'd seen enough of to last a lifetime.

He had to be cool. He had to be practical. He had to keep Marina at arm's length.

Just sex, von Kreus, he reminded himself as the sleep of forgetfulness washed over him.

This was just sex.

Chapter 5

Witt awoke resolved to repair the damage he'd done last night and lock his heart away, back where it belonged, away from Marina. Away from where it could hurt and be hurt. The lesson he'd learned at a tender age came back to grip him fiercely.

So, instead of nestling deeper into her body as he really wanted to do, he slid her from his arms as she slept and slipped out of bed. Luckily it was Saturday, so neither of them had to go in to work. It wouldn't hurt to let her sleep while he got his head together.

He went first for a shower, then padded to the spare bedroom, which he'd turned into his office, and flipped on the computer.

Watching it boot up and go through its daily safety

routines, he had to grip the arms of his leather office chair to keep from jumping up and running straight back to bed. Damn, he still wanted her! And damn that shower for rinsing the scent of her from his skin. If he couldn't have the real thing, at least he could have—

Suddenly, a sharp beeping sound came from his computer. A bright green screen lit up showing a series of frequency graphs. He hit the mute button so Marina wouldn't wake, frowning at the screen. Then let out a low oath.

According to the graphs, there was an electronic bug somewhere in the flat that hadn't been here yesterday morning.

Quickly he grabbed the portable scanner that would detect where the transmitter had been planted, and waved the wand over every square inch of his office. Nothing. Searching systematically through the flat, he found the signal in the living room. Coming from the marble-topped coffee table. Originating inside of Marina's purse.

He debated for a nanosecond before dumping its contents onto the table. One item at a time, he tested for the bug. It was in her mobile phone.

Good God. Someone was bugging Marina's phone.

He swiftly replaced the other things in her purse, then went back to his office and carefully took the mobile apart. He found a miniature transmitter hidden in the battery compartment. He stared at it for several minutes wondering what the hell to do. If he took it out, whoever had her under surveillance would know they'd been made. Their next method of finding out what they wanted to know from Marina might not be as benign as a bug. But who had planted it?

Camara and the diamond gang?

Whoever shot at her outside the hotel?

Someone from a different mission he didn't know about?

Yessus. What to do?

His first move was obvious. He grabbed his digital camera and took several macro shots of the transmitter, then closed up the phone and replaced it in her purse. Opening up his e-mail program, he uploaded the photos to the Lazlo Group's ftp site. After scanning his own secure phone, he dialed Corbett Lazlo's private number.

"Hey, *howzit boikie?* I thought this was your day off."

"No rest for the wicked," Witt replied, which got him a chuckle. "Listen, I found something interesting." He told his boss about Marina's hidden transmitter. "I've sent you pictures. Can you get one of the tech guys to identify the type of bug and where it came from?"

"Sure thing." But Corbett couldn't hide his surprise. Everyone knew that from its inception MI6 had always been downright paranoid about electronic surveillance. "This is disturbing. SIS issues their operatives new untraceable, disposable mobiles every few weeks to cut down on the possibility of being bugged or tracked through them."

"Which means whoever it was must have done it recently."

"Exactly."

"You think Marina's in danger?"

Corbett was silent for a moment. "Probably not. A bug means whoever is listening or tracking her wants her alive and working her op. They're after information."

"I'd better tell her."

"No. Not yet," Corbett warned. "If she stops talking, they'll notice. Let our techs find out who it is before we decide what to do."

"But what if it's Camara? She could be in real danger if he knows she works for MI6."

"Do you really think he'd have set up the interrogation last night if he knew about her and therefore you, as well?"

"We don't have proof that Claude's boss is Camara."

"Do you have reason to doubt it?"

Witt blew out a breath. "No, but I still don't like keeping Marina in the dark."

"Noted. Don't worry, she's a good agent. She won't say anything on that phone she shouldn't." There was another pause. "Witt, have there been any other unusual incidents happening to you? Like the shooting, I mean. Anyone following you? That kind of thing?"

"We were followed back to my place last night after I talked with you, but it was one of Claude's crew, a low-life called Deco, checking up on us. Marina stayed over to keep our cover intact with them." He'd already filled Corbett in on what went down at the interrogation. "Did you pick up Etienne and his mother?"

"Yes. She's been relocated, and we gave the kid a stern lecture and a number to call when Claude and the boys get in touch with him. He doesn't know who we are, only that we're keeping mama safe. Probably thinks we're French Special Branch."

They talked for several more minutes about the situation, the conversation all business. But there was an undertone to Corbett's voice that was so…unlike him, Witt almost couldn't place it. The boss actually sounded…anxious. Finally he asked, "Is there something else going on, boss? You seem distracted."

Corbett cleared his throat. "I got another e-mail this morning."

Witt swore. "What did it say?"

"Just two words. 'Ready, set…'"

Hell. "*Yessus,* another threat."

"Be careful, Witt. Be very careful. I'm back to thinking that shooting the other day may have been aimed at you and not Marina."

He thought about it but couldn't agree. "No. The guy was an amateur. Whoever's threatening the Lazlo Group are professionals. Their bombs, their guns, their e-mails, have all proved untraceable."

"We couldn't trace the bullets or casings we collected from your shooting, either. Standard nine-mil Luger ammo, available anywhere in the world. No rifling match in any database in Europe or the States."

Double hell. This was new information. "That only means he used a new gun. Any luck with the photo I took of the shooter? Were you able to ID him?"

"No joy. The tech guys ran the photo through the facial-recognition software and compared it to every criminal database we could access. No one popped. The kid has no record."

"Damn. A virgin with a new gun. Who the hell is this wanker?"

"Wish I knew. Wish I even knew for sure who his target was."

"Me, too. Sorry, boss. If I hadn't been so focused on protecting Marina I'm sure I could have caught him."

"You, unfocused? That's not like you."

"Tell me about it," he muttered.

The pause this time was filled with unspoken meaning. "Witt. Is there something you aren't reporting? Something more than a cover going on between you two?"

Witt hesitated, but only for a fraction of a second. "Nothing to worry about, boss."

He could almost hear Corbett's eyebrows shoot up. "Damn it, not you, too! I just lost two of my best agents to the unholy state of matrimony. I need you with your mind clear and on the job. Especially with all this crap coming down on us."

"The job's always my first priority. You know that," Witt assured him.

"Yeah, yeah. That's what they said, too."

"Corbett. Trust me. I'm not getting married. Ever."

There was a sound in the doorway. Witt whirled, reaching for his gun. He realized simultaneously that he wasn't wearing his shoulder holster, and that it was Marina in the doorway.

"Gotta go, boss," he said, and snapped his phone shut. "Hi."

"Hi."

She had wrapped the sheet around her but was obviously still naked under it. She looked sleepy and pink and disheveled and sexy as all hell. He was instantly hard, his body's conditioned response to the sight and scent of her, just from their one night of unbridled sexual intimacy.

"What are you doing?" she asked, peering at the computers so she missed his reaction. A shade of uncertainty clouded her eyes. As though she'd expected him to be there in bed when she awoke, and when he wasn't, she didn't know what else might be different this morning. She hung back, not moving any closer.

How much of his conversation with Corbett had she heard?

"Just, um…" He waved his mobile at the equipment on the desk. "Checking in with the boss. And doing my usual morning security check."

Her gaze slid to him. "Is everything all right?"

"Sure," he said.

God, this was awkward.

She nodded and turned into the hall. "I'd better get going."

"Why? The jewelry shop is closed today."

He caught a glimpse of her profile. She was nibbling her bottom lip. "I, um…I just have to go."

"No, you don't. What's wrong?" He had a sinking feeling that he knew the answer.

"I'm sorry. This is not working for me. I just can't do it." She hurried off toward the bedroom.

"Marina!" *Verdomme.* Damn it to hell. "Wait!"

He ran after her but was too late. She was already in the en suite bathroom with the door locked. He knocked.

"Go away. I'm getting dressed."

Screw that. He kicked the door in, breaking the lock. She stood clutching last night's pink outfit to her chest, her Glock in her hand pointed at him.

"Gonna shoot me, *skat?* Put it away."

After a wary look at the smashed door, she lowered the weapon. "Sorry. Reflex. What the hell, Witt?"

"You wouldn't open the door," he said reasonably.

Her eyebrows flicked. "Remind me never to piss you off."

"Ditto." They stared at each other for several heartbeats.

"What do you want?"

Now there was a loaded question. What *did* he want? Sex? Breakfast? A picket fence? Suddenly he wasn't so sure anymore. But one thing he did know.

"I want you to stay."

She shook her head. "Last night was such a bad idea I can't believe I ever let you talk me into it. I have to get out of here."

He'd thought last night was a great idea. It was this morning that had gone pear shaped. He crossed his arms over his chest and blocked what was left of the bathroom door, feeling mulishly stubborn. "You are not going anywhere."

Her eyes narrowed. She reached up and poked him in the chest with a finger. "*You* were the one who left the bed, stud. Not me. You can't have it both ways."

"We talked about this last night. What's changed?"

"No, *you* talked about it, Witt. I never agreed to your terms. You just caught me in a weak moment. The fact is, I can't deal with a just-sex kind of relationship. And neither of us wants any more than that. So leaving is pretty much the only option here."

"No."

Her teeth gritted. "Then what do you suggest?"

He knew what he'd like to suggest. Something that entailed grabbing her and hauling her back to bed. He'd been a fool to let her wake without him. What had he been thinking?

He'd been trying to distance himself, that's what. Get his perspective back. Shake the feeling that for the first time since Sarah died, his world had been turned upside down.

Yeah, good luck with that.

"I suggest you get dressed and then we can grab breakfast somewhere." There. A decision.

She held out her pink miniskirt and cut-up T-shirt. "In these? I don't think so."

Once decided, he would not be deterred. "I'll lend

you some clothes. Something's bound to fit. More or less." He walked to the bedroom bureau. "You'd better start keeping a change of clothes here."

She stared at him incredulously. "Have you been listening to a word I've said? I am so not—"

"Whatever happens—or doesn't happen—in that bed, we're still working together, Marina. Our cover is that we're an engaged couple. Last night proved it to them. We can't change horses now."

He pulled a soft pair of jeans from his drawer and tossed them at her. Then he went to his closet and snagged a white dress shirt off a hanger. He followed her back into the bathroom and pressed it into her reluctant hands.

She looked angry. And something else… Scared? Maybe. He didn't blame her. He was feeling more than a bit unsure himself. Sex, breakfast or picket fence? This was completely unknown territory. Apparently for both of them.

He reached up and took her face between his hands, then he kissed her. She tried to pull away, but he didn't let her. He didn't kiss her hard, but he did kiss her persuasively. He kissed her until at last she gave in and responded.

When he finally let her go, she looked down at the floor. "I don't want this," she murmured.

"I don't, either," he confessed. "But we both deal in facts. And the fact is, this is the way it is between us. We can't ignore it."

"I can."

"Do I really have to show you how wrong you are?"

Her cheeks turned pink, but her chin went up. "You're a bloody bastard, you know that?"

"Old news, babe. Now, we can either have breakfast, or we can go back to bed. Your choice."

From the look on her face he figured she was contemplating a third alternative—one that involved the Glock.

"There's a tough one," she snapped, turned and spun the shower faucets full on.

He sighed, knowing that from the moment he'd opened his eyes that morning he'd totally screwed up. He was terrible at this touchy-feely stuff. Another reason he avoided relationships. Strangely, this time it actually bothered him. It never had before.

He slipped his arms around her from behind, gently tugging her stiff body against his chest. "Marina, please. I'm an idiot, I know that. I want it to be good between us. Just tell me what you need, and I'll give it to you. Anything."

"I already did, Witt. I need you to leave me alone. Quit the op and go away."

"Not going to happen," he murmured in her hair. He softened his embrace, caressing her with his hands. She'd dropped the clothes but still held the sheet clutched around her. He could feel the heat of her body through the bunched-up fabric. The musky scent of their lovemaking drifted up from it. It aroused him. He didn't hide his reaction, but he didn't push it, either. Not what she needed at the moment.

"Witt, stop," she whispered. But her muscles started to relax, her body slowly melting in his arms.

"You still want me as much as I want you," he said. "Why won't you just admit that?"

"I will," she said. "I do. That's not the problem."

"Then what is?" he asked with mounting frustration.

She sighed out a long breath. "You say you're not afraid of a woman's love. But you *are* afraid. If you weren't, you wouldn't have left the bed this morning. You wouldn't want a just-sex relationship. You wouldn't be afraid to have feelings for the woman you're sleeping with."

He turned her in his arms, peering into her eyes. "What are you saying?"

She jetted out a breath. "I'm saying I can't do just sex. You'll have to accept that. But anything more would complicate our lives too much, so please just let me go."

They seemed to be going around in circles. Neither of them wanted to give in. He sure as hell didn't. He gave it one more shot.

"We've already made love, *skat*. All night. It's too late to pull back now. The damage has been done."

Her lips curved into a humorless smile. "Spoken like a true man."

Now he was mystified. "What?"

She shook her head. "I'm taking a shower." She dropped the sheet onto the floor and stepped under the spray.

He shoved his hands in his jeans pockets and watched her, a scowl creasing his forehead. Yeah, that was another reason he avoided relationships. Female logic. Now, there was an oxymoron.

He wanted to join her in the shower. His palms itched to take the soap from her and slather it all over her body. His fingers yearned to massage shampoo through her hair until the bubbles flowed down the curve of her neck and her back and over her pretty bottom. His— Yeah, well, never mind the rest of his body. Best not to think about what those parts craved to do to her.

He stalked out of the en suite and paced around the living room, trying to find the objectivity he'd lost somewhere between leaving the bed this morning and finding that stupid bug in her phone.

Yeah, he wanted sex with her. Lots of it. There was no denying it. But that wasn't all. He had this overwhelming urge to tuck her under his arm and pull his gun, to protect her from all comers. It made him furious that someone was targeting her. It made him crazy to know that when she walked out of his flat someone could be out there waiting for her. Just to listen to her conversations? Or to kill her?

He needed to find out who the hell it was.

He needed to be there to make sure she was safe.

And somehow, some way, he needed to figure out how he could keep her in his bed. And in his life. Because in all this confusion, one thing was becoming abundantly clear.

He was not prepared to let her go.

Not yet.

Hell, maybe not ever.

* * *

"Thanks for breakfast," Marina told Witt when they'd finished their crepes and lattes at a small café a few blocks from his place.

He'd been acting strange all through the meal. Quiet. Snippy when he did speak. No doubt he was angry because she wouldn't sleep with him anymore. She'd tried to explain her decision to him, but he refused to see reason. He couldn't seem to wrap his mind around the idea that she could think sex with him was amazing and mind-blowing but still not want to do it again. He didn't get that it was *because* it was amazing and mind-blowing that she didn't want to do it again. She was already falling for him. She had to nip those feelings in the bud before someone got hurt. Like her.

With their jobs, any relationship was a recipe for disaster. Especially one where deep feelings were involved. She'd seen the hell her parents had gone through on that score.

No, thanks.

A spy had no business falling in love. She wasn't about to let herself go down that path to pain.

"I'll see you at the shop on Monday," she said, and turned determinedly toward the Métro stop.

He grabbed her arm. "Hold on. Where are you going?"

"I have to get to my embassy. I always check in with Vauxhall Cross on Saturday mornings."

Vauxhall Cross was where SIS headquarters were located, in an imposing and distinctive ziggurat style building overlooking the Thames in London. It was

pretty funny that one of the most high-profile buildings in England housed the nation's most secretive
organization.

"Video conference?" he asked.

She nodded. "Thank goodness for technology. I
prefer dealing directly with the brass, not some
middleman."

"Your section chief is James Dalgliesh, right?"

She shot him a withering look. "I'd tell you but
then I'd have to kill you."

He returned the look. "Very funny. I'm to report to
him, too. We're working this op together, remember?"

If only she could forget.

She'd planned on stopping at her place to change
out of her borrowed clothes, but didn't want Witt
tagging along. Frankly, she didn't trust herself alone
with him. Last night was still vividly imprinted on
her body. On her senses. On her imagination. She
didn't think she could resist him if he got it in his
mind to seduce her again. She wasn't being wishy-
washy, just realistic. So far she was 0-2 against his
advances. Not a great track record.

Better to skip the temptation and just endure the
teasing from her friends on the embassy staff for
wearing his jeans and shirt.

"We'll take my car," he said.

She rolled her eyes. At least she was wearing her
own bra.

They drove to a car park close to the British
embassy on rue du Faubourg St. Honoré. They left

Witt's Land Rover on the bottom level, then walked through a secure tunnel to the underground entrance and made their way to a second-floor video-conferencing room.

Apparently Dalgliesh had already met Witt on some past operation, so no introductions were necessary once they'd made the video link with Vauxhall Cross. Marina gave her progress report for the past week, and answered several follow-up questions about the shooting incident and their meeting with Claude and the other Africans last night.

"I'm confident Claude works for Abayomi Camara. I expect a meeting with him any day."

Dalgliesh was impressed with their progress.

"Glad to have you onboard, von Kreus," he told Witt when the conversation turned his way. "Marina was the only one of my people with the requisite skills to pull off the boutique position, but these African diamond dealers tend to be a macho lot. They don't trust women as readily as men. Your background is perfect for infiltrating their cartel."

"The Lazlo Group is always happy to help our friends at MI6," Witt responded, using what Marina figured must be his company PR smile. "And I have a personal interest in seeing these terrorists go down. I hate the misery they're causing in Africa. They should all be behind bars or six feet under."

His posture was casual, sitting at the conference table with one leg resting across his thigh, leaning an elbow on the polished wood surface of the table. But when he said that last bit his eyes took on the hard, concentrated focus of a warrior. He meant every word. Marina was very glad he was one of the good guys, on their side.

"I agree," Dalgliesh said. "Now that you two have actually penetrated Camara's Paris network, I want you to concentrate your efforts on getting close to the man himself."

"Marina's right, after last night, he'll want to meet us soon," Witt said. "I'm pretty sure we passed his test."

"Excellent. Your focus should be gathering evidence to arrest him. Abayomi Camara is the linchpin of the Angolan blood-diamond market and a player all over Africa. Mosaad took out his second in command a few months back, so with Camara out of the picture, too, the whole Angolan cartel should shut down and the rest be thrown into a bit of chaos. At least long enough for us or the Yanks to get a strike team in to clean up in the confusion."

"Are we looking for any particular type of evidence?" Marina asked.

"Information on their routes, their European contacts, modes of transport, all of that would be invaluable. But we need to catch Camara himself in possession of an actual shipment of illegal diamonds, or find hard evidence linking him to them. Without that, his arrest won't stick. That is your mission."

"Works for me," Witt said.

"I'm sure I don't need to say it," Dalgliesh added, "but your orders are to bring him down alive. I don't care what he does, don't kill him. Deputy Director Milleflora wants a chance to debrief the bastard. Camara's sitting on a ton of information that we could use."

"You mean like names of corrupt African government officials," Witt said, eyes narrowing.

"For starters."

Marina was beginning to suspect why Witt had wanted in on this operation so badly. He may be an African expatriate, but he loved the continent of his birth, that much was patently obvious. She felt a trickle of shame that she'd thought he had horned in just to get close to her. How egotistical could she get? Witt von Kreus was a patriot. A hero of his country. And he was paying for his beliefs by living his life in exile, half a world away from everything he loved. She wondered if she would have that kind of dedication if their roles were reversed.

Her admiration of him skyrocketed once again. The man had unsuspected depths.

"Marina?" Dalgliesh said with a raised brow. It clearly wasn't the first time he'd said her name.

She startled back to the present. "Yes, sir?"

"Any questions?"

"No, sir."

"All right, then. Good luck to both of you. Same time next week." With that, the video feed went blank.

Marina stood and gathered her things, and Witt did likewise. She went to a console at the back of the room and ejected the DVD recording of the meeting, which was always automatically made.

"I just have to pouch this and send it to London."

He nodded and trailed after her to the mail room. "Who sees it?" She shot him a glance. "Just curious," he said, lifting a shoulder.

"As far as I know, one copy goes to Deputy Director Milleflora—Dalgliesh's boss—and another goes to Archives," she answered absently. "Probably gets copied onto some mega hard drive by some geek in the basement, never to be viewed again."

"Unless something blows up."

"Yeah. But that isn't going to happen, is it? We're going to nail this bad guy and throw away the key."

"You bet," he agreed with a smile. "And speaking of keys. We should stop and have a spare of my flat key made for you."

She stopped in midstride and spun on a toe to face him. "Excuse me?"

"Probably should make me one of yours, too."

Scandalized, she dropped her jaw. "Witt, are you living in some alternate universe or something? There's no way you're getting a key to my flat."

He shrugged again. "Whatever. You'll still need one for mine."

"No."

"We're supposed to be a couple. Engaged, remember? Fiancées exchange keys," he said calmly.

"It's a security breach. Your boss won't like it."

"He's the one who suggested it."

She closed her eyes and counted to ten. No way in hell did she want a key to Witt von Kreus's bedroom—er, home. That implied a level of intimacy she was *so* not comfortable with she was ready to run screaming out of here and not look back.

But she couldn't do that, could she? Because he was right, the rotter. If Claude or Camara got curious and started poking around in their personal lives, it would look very strange if one of them didn't have a key to the other's place.

"All right. Fine," she said. "But I'm not going to use it."

Witt just smiled.

And her heart did a slow, spinning leap off the edge of panic. She just prayed that when it landed, it would still be in one piece.

Chapter 6

"How long have you been assigned to Paris?" Witt asked Marina as they headed back to the car.

"Just under a month," she replied.

He glanced at her and took a wild guess. "I'll bet it's been all work and no play." She didn't seem the type to indulge in frivolous pastimes like sightseeing. At least on her own.

"What's that supposed to mean?"

He grinned. "Have you been to the Louvre?"

She pursed her lips. "Haven't had time yet."

"The Champs Elysée? The Arc de Triomphe?"

"I saw them from the bus once." When he gave her a smirk, she said defensively. "It drove the whole way up the Champs Elysée."

"Eiffel Tower?"

She scowled at him. "I'm not here to play tourist, Witt. I actually have a job to do."

He hooked his arm around hers and swung her in a 180, the opposite direction from the car park. "Then let's do it today."

"Do what?" she asked, trying to tug her arm back.

"Play tourist. I'll show you the Arc de Triomphe. You really shouldn't miss it."

"But I've seen—"

"Not from the top, you haven't."

She frowned. "I didn't even know you could get up there."

"Most people don't," he said. "It's the best-kept secret in Paris." The top of the Arc was one of his favorite spots. A great view of the city and no crowds, just a trickle of intrepid travelers who didn't mind a long climb up a narrow stairway. "Come on. My treat. Besides, what else do you have to do today?"

"Laundry?"

But she didn't resist when he laced his fingers through hers and steered them toward the Place de la Concorde Métro stop. Progress.

Since it was the weekend, the Métro was crowded with shoppers from the suburbs and throngs of tourists chattering in a half-dozen languages, so they had to stand. Witt wrapped his arms around Marina and held on to the center pole two-fisted as the Métro tram barreled along, vibrations shooting through his legs and body. Or was that because of her nearness?

Around them, the dusty, distinctive metallic smell of the underground mingled with the sweet, flowery fragrance of her shampoo and her soft skin. He could stand like this forever, just holding her close and breathing her in.

Their stop came all too quickly. They jostled off and made their way above ground to the impressive stone monument, then he ushered her into the well-hidden entrance to a circular stairway that led up to the observation deck on top of the arch.

The stairs going up went on forever. Not that he was complaining. He walked behind Marina, and the view from that perspective was pretty great, too. The jeans he'd lent her fitted just a shade snug on her. Okay, they were downright tight. He liked how her backside looked in them. A lot. Too bad she was wearing a jacket—his, too—so he only caught an occasional glimpse of the full effect.

Halfway up she stopped at one of the few postage stamp-size landings. "Good grief. Are we almost there?"

She was in good shape, so she wasn't breathing too hard, but there was a sheen of moisture on her forehead.

"I can see I'll need to take you out running," he teased.

She made a face. "Smart aleck."

He moved in and grasped her around the waist, nuzzling her neck. "Or maybe we can find a more pleasant mode of exercise."

She wriggled free of him, holding him at arm's length, though it was impossible for her to escape completely without falling down the narrow stairway. But she was smiling. "You have a one-track mind, von Kreus."

He grinned and trapped her against the rough, gray wall. "It's what makes me so good at my job. You may as well give it up and surrender, *skat*. I always get what I'm after."

She winked and slid under his arm, trotting up the stairs and around the bend, out of sight. "So do I, von Kreus," came echoing down the stairwell. "So do I."

He chuckled. They'd see about that. He had no intention of losing this one. This woman. Somewhere along the line, he'd resolved himself. He wanted her. He wanted to keep her. No, not forever. But for longer than one night.

She appealed to him in so many ways, he felt an intense need to explore their connection further. Much further. She was in the same business as he, so she'd understand his background. She wouldn't hold it against him. Just for an affair, at any rate. It would be a different story if she were looking for a more permanent relationship. Then he wouldn't be the kind of man she'd be interested in pursuing. What sane woman would want a bloke with his baggage? None. Hell, his own mother didn't understand what he'd done, what he was still doing.

But he could make Marina happy in the short run. At the very least until the Camara operation was over and she was reassigned somewhere else in the world.

Until she left Paris, he was her man.

He sprinted up the stairs after her. It was a long way up, and she didn't let him catch her. The closer he got, the faster she went. They were both laughing and panting hard by the time they reached the top and burst out into the bright fall sunshine. The crisp, cool air hit his heated skin, but it didn't touch the heat inside his body.

He grabbed her and swung her around in his arms. "Gotcha."

She put hers around his neck and hugged him back, laughter spilling from her lips. "I let you catch me."

"So you must like me a little."

"Nah. There's just nowhere else to run."

He glanced around as he twirled her. A couple of Europeans were in the tiny gift shop next to them, but none were paying any attention. A clutch of Asian tourists standing at the small History of Napoleon exhibit pointed at them and giggled. One brought out an instamatic and aimed it their way, so Witt ducked his head and kissed Marina, setting her on her feet with their faces averted from the lens.

"Camera," he murmured, still breathing hard.

She played along when he changed angles, and let him deepen the kiss. His body reacted, recalling other scenes of breathlessness and sweat-damp skin they'd shared last night.

She pulled away, sliding her hands from his neck to push gently at his shoulders. "That wasn't fair."

"Who said anything about fair?" He gave her a final kiss, slung his arm around her and they walked a slow circuit around the edge of the observation deck.

As always the view was amazing. The Paris city panorama was high enough to be above every other rooftop, but close enough to the ground that details were easy to make out. The sky was a clear cerulean blue, the sun a bright-yellow orb that bathed the entire city in glittering sparkles. It must have been on a day like today that the Sun King Louis XIV chose his personal emblem. It was enough to inspire the gods.

"Beautiful," Marina breathed reverently when they'd gone all the way around. "What an incredible place." She kissed his cheek. "Thank you for bringing me."

"My pleasure. What's next? Top of the Eiffel Tower?"

To his chagrin, his mobile phone chose that moment to vibrate in his pocket. He checked the number on the screen. It was Corbett.

"Damn. Hold on." He punched the on button. "Witt here."

"Just thought I'd let you know, we got some info on that electronic device you found in Marina's mobile," Corbett responded without preamble.

"Tell me."

"It functions both as a bug and a tracking device. Strangely enough, it's a model predominantly used by the Brits. SIS, to be exact."

"So it wasn't Camara." Witt shot a glance at Marina, who had walked over to lean against the guardrail and soak in the view, then whispered, "But why would SIS want to bug one of their own officers?" He took several steps away from her so she wouldn't hear the conversation.

"It gets more interesting. It's also the same type of device found in a car belonging to an Interpol agent who turned up dead several weeks ago in London."

Witt's blood ran cold. "Is there a connection?"

"Possibly. I have it on good authority that the agent was neck-deep in an investigation of a certain British attorney, our old friend Barrett Jenkins."

"Are you serious?" Barrett Jenkins was one of the fishy connections they'd discussed in relation to Jared Williams and Randy Kruger, the diamond courier who'd been killed at the bombing of the Lazlo Group headquarters in Rome last month. "So we aren't the only ones who suspect Jenkins of being shady."

"It gets better—or worse, depending on how you look at it. Turns out another one of attorney Jenkins's clients is Abayomi Camara."

Witt swore softly. "There's the link we've been looking for."

"I agree. But here's where it gets complicated," Corbett continued. "Jenkins is also the attorney of record for none other than John Breckenridge, a senior MP who sits on the British Finance Committee. Breckenridge recently gave Interpol a statement in support of Jenkins."

Witt's jaw clenched. "Okay, this is officially getting ugly."

"Maybe. Maybe not," Corbett prevaricated. "Jenkins undoubtedly cultivated strong client ties to the government, hoping to escape scrutiny on his dirty dealings with Camara. Or others."

"Which could mean Breckenridge has no knowledge of his activities and is completely innocent."

"Exactly. Naturally, I briefed the PM. He has asked me to start a hush-hush full-scale investigation into this whole affair. Especially the link to Breckenridge."

Yessus. Witt took a moment to digest it all, then asked, "Where does that leave Marina?"

Corbett blew out a breath. "I'm not sure. It doesn't have to mean anything at all. The transmitter in her phone could easily be part of a routine internal countercheck SIS runs on all its officers, nothing to do with any of this."

"It could also have been put there for Camara, by someone within SIS. The way it's looking, Jared Williams's SIS contact—the superior he was giving the information Chloe fed him—that contact must surely be working for Camara, too."

"It would still make no sense for him to bug Marina. If that scenario were true, Camara would already know she works for SIS and would not have set foot in the boutique while she was there, or let Claude near her."

"You're right," Witt said, immensely relieved. *Thank God.*

"What about her section chief? James Dalgliesh. Could he have planted it?"

Witt considered, then shook his head. "I don't think so. We did an op together a few years back and he seems straight as an arrow. Besides, Dalgliesh sent her on this mission, and she gives him constant updates. There'd be no need for him to track her."

"True." There was a pause. "You don't think Marina could have put the bug there herself, that she could be a double agent of some kind?"

"Not possible." The thought was preposterous. "Impossible."

"No, of course she isn't. But it had to be asked."

"The question is why someone in SIS would bug her phone at all? She sends a DVD of all her meetings with Dalgliesh to the Archives at Vauxhall Cross. Any high-level officer could access them. Just as with Camara, there'd be no need for a bug."

"The evidence suggests," said Corbett thoughtfully, "that if it's connected at all, the device was planted by a single individual simply as a precaution. An instant early warning if something is about to go down on the op, rather than waiting for the reports. Some who is nervous she's about to arrest Camara. This is someone who wants firsthand information on her movements. So he can flee if and when she gets too close."

"That makes more sense," Witt admitted, not liking where this was going. "Or like you said, it could have nothing to do with this operation at all."

"Well, I'll keep digging, and let you know if anything else turns up."

"Thanks."

"And, Witt. Don't tell Marina about the transmitter yet. She'd have to report it to her boss, and Dal-

gliesh would pull her phone for sure. But if our
theory is correct and Camara really has infiltrated
SIS, then that bug can be used to expose the mole.
Lead them into a trap. For the time being, just keep
her safe."

Troubled, Witt reluctantly consented, rang off and
slid his phone back in his pocket.

Yessus. This was not good. No way did he want
Marina in the middle of all this. It was crazy dangerous.

"Who was that?" Marina asked from behind him.

He turned, making himself smile. "Lazlo. Just
an update on a case I closed last month. Nothing
important."

He hated to lie to her. But Corbett was right.
Better to wait until all the facts were in. And in the
meantime stick to her like a bad sunburn. What harm
could she come to, if he was with her 24/7?

He didn't want to think about that.

She tilted her head. "Okay," she said. He could tell
she didn't believe him but wasn't going to push it.

His smile morphed to genuine. How had he gotten
so lucky? Gorgeous, smart, sexy and she respected
their professional boundaries without prodding or
pouting. The woman was as close to perfect as it got.

"Did I hear something about the Eiffel Tower?"
she asked cheerfully.

"Aha! You do like playing tourist."

"Truthfully, I love seeing the sights. I just hate
doing it by myself," she said as they made their way
back to the stairs. "Coming to places like this alone

when I'm on assignment just reminds me how much I miss my friends back home."

They entered a mezzanine level where a photo exhibit was on display, complete with benches and a few stray tourists. Witt pulled her into an embrace and kissed her.

"I know what you mean. I've been living on my own for a long time, but I still miss my parents and mates back in the old country. It's nice sharing the day with you." He put his face to her hair and his lips to her ear and whispered, "And the night was even nicer."

It took her several long heartbeats before she whispered back, "Yes, it was," but then she pulled out of his embrace. "We should get moving," she said, "if we're going to see everything today."

"What's the rush?" he called after her as she disappeared into the stairwell. "We've got lots of time to see the sights together." Days. Weeks. Months. At least, if he had anything to say about it.

"I'm in the mood now!" her disembodied voice floated back with a laugh.

Beauty. He trotted after her down the steep, circular stairs, catching up with her at the same microscopic landing they'd halted on going up.

He pulled her into an embrace. "Hey, I'm in the mood, too," he murmured with a wide grin as she squirmed and giggled in his arms. Of course, around her he was always in the mood. "How about here?"

He flicked the button on her jeans waistband with his thumb. Teasing, of course. But it popped open.

Her eyes widened. "Witt! We can't. Someone might come!"

He waggled his eyebrows. "Damn, I hope so."

She choked on a laugh, batting at his hands. "You are incorrigible."

"I do my best."

Suddenly a whining buzz whizzed past his ear, followed by a pop in the stone wall about six steps above them. A puff of dust exploded from the spot, followed by another pop and puff on the opposite wall still farther up. It took him less than a second to realize what it was and react.

He swore loudly, pushed Marina to the floor and shouted, "Stay down!" as he spun and vaulted down the stairs at top speed, chasing the bastard who'd just shot at them. Again.

But the little creep was fast. Witt could hear him running the whole way to the bottom, ten steps ahead and always just out of sight in the circular stairwell. He wanted to shout, "You better run, you little shit, because if I catch you I'll tear you limb from limb!" but he needed to save his lungs for breathing. He thought about sending a few bullets down to stop the blighter, but no way. Not in a public place. Witt had strict rules about endangering innocent bystanders.

At the bottom of the stairs he flew out into the open area under the arch and whirled a circle to try to spot the shooter.

There!

A man glanced up as he hurried down the steps to the Métro tunnel. Young. Tall. Blond. It was the same kid that had boarded the bus after the hotel shooting! Witt sped after him. But by the time he got there, the man had disappeared into the maze of underground pedestrian and Métro tunnels. People eyed Witt warily when he let out a string of curses, and gave him a wide berth.

Verdomme!

He bent over and grabbed his knees, sucking much-needed oxygen into his lungs while he got his muscles and his fury under control.

Whoever the blond guy was, the wanker was toast. Witt would hunt him down like the rat he was and make him wish he'd never been born.

"You okay?" Winded, Marina halted next to him and matched his bent-over pose, catching her breath, too.

No. He wasn't okay.

He was dead furious and wanted to kill someone. Badly. Preferably the man trying to shoot Marina, but at this point he was so angry just about anyone would do.

Which was why he wasn't okay. He didn't *get* angry like this. He never got emotional during a case; he was always the cool one, the consummate professional. Until *this* case.

"Yeah," he said through gritted teeth. "Just fine and dandy."

She slanted him a raised eyebrow. "Right."

"It was the same guy," he said.

She straightened. "As the hotel?"

"Yep." He straightened, too, hands on hips. "We need to find out who he is."

"And which one of us he's shooting at."

"Not to mention why."

"In other words, square one." She sighed. "But how do we ID him? Didn't you say Corbett searched every database in Europe and the States and came up empty?"

He blew out a breath to a calming count of ten. "We just have to dig deeper. Expand the search outside law enforcement. I'll get Corbett to put someone on it full-time."

"He'll do that?"

"The Lazlo Group has lost four agents in two months. If the shooter is targeting me, Corbett will do whatever he needs to in order to track down those responsible."

"And if it's me?"

"Corbett is good friends with your father," he reminded her.

She nodded her complete understanding. Nothing more needed to be said. The national security game was a small world. Those on the same side took care of each other, at least when there were personal ties. And it didn't get more personal than saving a man's daughter.

"We'd better get back to the Arc and preserve the scene," she said. "The forensics might tell us something."

"I'll call Lazlo and get a team here asap."

"Could be tricky. Foreign jurisdiction. Important national monument."

He followed her out of the tunnels. "Not a problem. Trust me, the boss has friends in high places."

Very high. Ten minutes after Witt spoke with

Corbett, a *commissaire* of the French National Police arrived with five uniformed officers in tow. The Arc de Triomphe rooftop and stairway was roped off for forty-five minutes while the Lazlo Group forensics team went over every inch of stone, metal, glass and cement inside and on top.

The only evidence they found was two bullets, both battered beyond usefulness from multiple ricochets off the hard stone walls of the stairwell. The bullets were, however, of the same make and caliber as those found outside the hotel three days earlier. Nine-mil Lugers.

Not a lot to go on. But when you had squat to begin with, every little bit helped.

Corbett put in a brief appearance at the scene, quietly kibbutzing off to the side with the French *commissaire* for a few minutes. Politics. The boss played it well, which was why Lazlo agents were allowed into places all over the world that most law enforcement agencies only dreamed of. Witt himself had been to nearly every royal and presidential palace around the globe, working secret assignments for their owners. Since joining the Lazlo Group, his clients had been Hollywood stars, blue-blooded aristocrats, industrial magnates, professional athletes, sheikhs, sultans and billionaires. That on top of subcontracting out with the official security services of a dozen countries, as he was doing with the British SIS on this case.

It was a great life, filled with adventure, glitz and amazing financial reward.

But he would trade it all for the chance to wrap his fingers around the neck of one young, blond assassin and find out what the hell was going on. Because if anything happened to Marina on his watch, Witt would never forgive himself.

An hour after losing the shooter in the tunnels, they walked back to the car park and picked up the Land Rover.

"We'll see the Eiffel Tower another time," he promised. "Let's have dinner in tonight. My place. What do you say?"

She shot him a look as she buckled up. "Trying to babysit me again, von Kreus? Or just seduce me?"

Try both. He went for innocent. "Who, me?"

"Honestly, I don't—"

He held up his hands. "Whatever you're about to say, I know all that. I was just..."

Just what? Going crazy thinking about someone hurting her? Wanting desperately to protect her? Needing to wrap his arms around her all night so he knew she would be safe? All of the above?

"I was just hoping you wouldn't mind standing guard over me tonight. You know, a bad guy *is* trying to kill me, hey?" He smiled guilelessly.

She rolled her eyes but couldn't disguise the laughter under her ironic, "So now you think it's you he's after?"

"No." His smile slid from his face.

So did hers. She sighed. "I'm not afraid of this clown. I've fought tougher guys over the last chocolate chip cookie at Starbucks."

"Getting shot at doesn't bother you?"

"I wouldn't be very good at my job if it did."

True enough. "It could still be me he wants."

"But you don't believe that."

No. He didn't. Not after he found that bug in her phone. "I don't know what I believe. Except that we're better off facing whatever this is together. Until we nail this guy, I'll watch your back. And I trust you to watch mine. Deal?"

She gazed at him in all seriousness for several moments, then nodded once. "Okay. Deal."

His smile returned. "Good choice." A wave of relief purled through him. And anticipation. Another night with Marina. Beauty. He could use this. On all fronts.

Unfortunately, he wouldn't get the chance, because just then his cell rang. It was Claude.

"Hope you and Marina aren't busy tonight," Claude said. "My boss wants to meet you."

Chapter 7

Marina was amped. Adrenaline sprinted through her veins as she and Witt, with Claude in the back seat, waited in the Land Rover at the appointed place and time for Camara to show.

This was it. What she'd worked toward for weeks. The objective of her mission was close at hand.

The orders from Dalgliesh and DDG Milleflora were specific. Meet Abayomi Camara. Gain his trust. Find hard evidence on him that would lead to his arrest and conviction. Do not kill him under any circumstances.

Fine with her. Her name may be Bond, but any license to kill was just in the movies. She'd never killed a human being and would just as soon not start now if she could help it. If all went well, Camara would never know who had brought him down. A bullet in his chest might tip him off.

She shifted in her seat for the hundredth time, eager for their quarry to show.

"Damn, girl, you must have had one too many espressos this afternoon," Witt said, glancing over at her.

She gave him a look. "Just excited, sweetheart. This contact could be our ticket to the big-time, in case you hadn't noticed."

She was in character again. Tonight her outfit was black—for power—but just as brash as yesterday's: black leather Donna Karan miniskirt with black thigh-high stockings that stopped just shy of the skirt's hem, and another cut-up T-shirt that showed bits of her two-hundred-euro black bra in all the right places. Her Glock 23 was tucked in her Prada handbag. She was ready to rock.

"I noticed," Witt returned, eyes pinioning hers.

For a second she wasn't sure if he was referring to her remark or her outfit. Not that there was any doubt as to the latter. His eyes had nearly popped out when she'd emerged from her bedroom after changing. She figured it was the stockings. If Claude wondered about her change of persona from boring, uptight shopgirl to Witt's mini-skirted sidekick, he gave no indication. In fact, Claude hadn't stopped leering since they picked him up at the Gare du Nord. She was hoping the outfit would have a similar effect on Camara.

Men were so easy. Flash a little skin and they instantly lost every vestige of common sense, or caution, and underestimated her. Their mistake. Made her job so much easier.

She smiled and crossed her legs. "So, Claude. Any idea why your boss wants to meet us?"

Claude shrugged. "I just do as I'm told. But he was impressed with your work last night. The information you got from that kid has already proven useful."

"Really?" she asked, hoping he would elaborate.

But he just showed his teeth and shook his head. "Or so I've been told."

"He's late," Witt said, drumming his fingers on the steering wheel. He glanced up and down the empty street where they'd been instructed to wait. It was in another bad area on the outskirts of the city. The whole neighborhood was a portrait of neglect. Grimy buildings, the stench of refuse, the depressing artifacts of dead-end lives.

"Now who's antsy?" she chided.

"Why don't you climb on over here and we can wear off some of our impatience on each other?" he suggested, his gaze returning to hers.

She tipped her head and called his bluff. "Sure. Why not?"

She saw the brief flash of surprise in his blue eyes. Then he grinned and went for his seat belt. Luckily—or not?—headlights swept onto the pavement from a side street.

"You lose, stud," she said. "He's here."

"Later," Witt said with a wink.

A gleaming white limo glided down the street like a cruising shark and stopped nose to nose with the Land Rover. If they had to make a run for it, Witt would have to back up first. Smart bad guys.

The front doors of the limo opened and two giant guys with Uzis stepped out. African, she surmised from their blue-black features and the tribal scars on their faces. They looked ferocious. Like real warriors.

Witt put the Land Rover in reverse and backed it up several feet, then killed the engine and pocketed the keys before he and Claude climbed out. Smarter Witt.

She popped her door and sashayed out as well, coming to a halt at his side.

Claude approached the giant closest to him and greeted him with a few cheerful sentences in a melodic language she didn't recognize. The giant grinned as they shook hands heartily, his eyes flicking to her. She stuck out a hip and looked back at him, going for unimpressed.

The other giant went to the back limo door and opened it. Camara got out and approached, guarded carefully by the two goons. She and Witt shared a covert look of triumph. Camara at last!

"I've seen you before," he said, studying her after Claude made introductions.

"I'm a salesgirl at Glace Chaud," she said. "I believe I was there once when you came in."

He nodded slowly. "Yes. I remember. You were dressed differently. And had black hair."

She gave a wry smile. "Monsieur Henri is partial to the designer look."

His regard sharpened. "And what are you partial to, *mademoiselle?*"

"Money, *monsieur,*" she answered without hesitation.

He chuckled softly. "And hurting people, from what I hear?"

"I do what I have to do," she said.

"For money."

"That's right."

Camara's gaze slid to Witt. "And you, *monsieur?* What do you like?"

"I like making my woman happy," Witt answered blandly. His words were pleasant enough, but there was a distinct warning in his unsmiling eyes. A look that said "hands off her or you deal with me and you won't like it."

An unbidden shiver sifted through Marina's body at the way he had just declared possession of her. Her mind knew it was only part of their cover, but her body felt a primitive thrill at being claimed in such a deliberate manner.

She stepped closer and wrapped herself around his relaxed arm—the left one—clinging to it and nestling against his side. "You do make me happy, darling. You know that," she murmured, kissing him under his ear.

Camara observed every move, his gaze calculating. Abruptly he turned and walked back to the car, gesturing for them to follow. "Come. Join me for dinner and we will talk."

She met Witt's eyes briefly and he gave a slight

nod. They were both carrying—Witt's gun was in its usual place in his shoulder holster—and so far Camara had been nothing but polite. Well, except for the machine-gun-toting bodyguards, but that was to be expected.

Witt tossed the Land Rover keys to Claude and told him to follow. Not that it would do them any good if things went pear-shape. Claude's loyalties belonged to Camara. But better to have the car within striking distance.

Camara preceded them into the back of the limousine, and they slid in behind him. It was one of those long numbers that had two benches facing each other in the passenger compartment. Surprisingly, Camara chose the backward seat, leaving them the one facing forward. A polite monster?

After raising the dark-tinted barrier between them and the driver, he opened a chrome bar built into the side panel and pulled out a bottle of champagne. Marina recognized the label. Expensive. Very expensive.

"Nice," she murmured, taking a sip after he handed her a tall, narrow flute. "What's the occasion?"

Witt remained silent as he settled in next to her, his arm stretched out casually behind her on the seat back. He accepted a flute, but she noticed he didn't drink. Was he suspicious, or just avoiding drinking on the job? His face was completely neutral, giving away absolutely nothing. Maybe he just didn't like champagne.

"In my country, meeting new friends is always an

occasion for celebration," Camara said, raising his glass with a broad smile, the attentive, convivial host. He seemed so sincere she had to remind herself the guys in the front seat were packing Uzis and the man smiling at her had ruthlessly killed hundreds of innocent victims in his quest to rule the Angolan conflict diamond trade. At least according to SIS intel.

She touched her glass to his, and the delicate ring of pure crystal tinkled through the compartment. "To new friends."

Camara made small talk with her since Witt remained mute as the limo sped out of Paris and into the countryside. It was pretty and green along the two-lane road that led them farther and farther from the bustle of the city and the sprawl of the suburbs. They chatted and she sipped on her champagne, memorizing their route. They wound through the countryside, past clutches of cheerful cottages, carefully tended yards and vegetable plots, and through a patchwork quilt of woods and small fields. Their host made no attempt to conceal their direction or lose Claude following in the Land Rover.

Should she be worried? Probably. Still, despite her heightened vigilance and the low buzz of adrenaline in her veins, she didn't feel uneasy. The champagne? Maybe. But Witt didn't appear too concerned, either. Of course, who could tell? He wasn't playing good cop today. More like inscrutable cop.

After half an hour the limo turned in through an ornate black iron gate and spiraled up a low hill to a château at the top. When it came into view she gasped softly. Incredibly beautiful, the modest-size private château was fashioned like a miniature fairy-tale castle. Windows sparkled welcomingly, surrounded by fancy brickwork and intricate stone walls that soared up in steep peaks and crenellated turrets.

Not what she'd pictured for the home of a ruthless killer.

"Yours?" she asked. His file had made no mention of a home in France.

"Just bought it last year. Through an intermediary, of course. Do you like it?" he asked, seemingly pleased with her reaction.

"Gorgeous," she said on an awed sigh. No need to pretend. It truly was.

The inside was no less so. Polished antiques mingled with comfortable furniture, cozy pillows and cushy Oriental rugs. The artwork and tapestries on the walls were splendid and tasteful, but not overwhelming or pretentious. A professional decorator, perhaps?

"I chose everything myself," Camara said, as though reading her thoughts.

"Beautiful," she said. Sinking into a luxurious sofa in the main salon, she looked at the man with new eyes.

She shouldn't. Outward appearances were deceiving. There was no reason a person with an ugly soul couldn't have a stunning home, and vice versa. But seeing his home, it all seemed so incongruous with the horrors of what he had allegedly done to pay for it.

"You live in France permanently?" she asked. Something else that hadn't been in the file.

"Not yet. But I plan to soon."

A pretty, young African girl dressed in colorful batik garb carried in a tray with a cut-glass decanter and three small, stemmed glasses. Her feet were bare. "Dinner will be ready in fifteen minutes, sir," she told Camara shyly.

"Thank you, Dina."

Marina watched her pad out again, thinking she looked healthy and happy and not the least bit nervous in Camara's presence.

Again he seemed to read her mind. "Dina is an orphan from a village in the north of my country," he said as he poured and handed around glasses of sherry. "Government soldiers killed her parents, along with most of the other villagers, so they could use their homes for a base of operations. Dina hid in the jungle with a few other children, and survived for ten days before they were discovered. When the soldiers moved on, the boys were forced to go with them as slaves. The girls were raped and left for dead. A French priest found them. Dina lived, but her sister wasn't so lucky. That was two years ago. She was fourteen at the time."

Marina swallowed, and glanced at the door through which the girl had disappeared. Her heart squeezed. The poor thing. "That's terrible," she murmured.

"It is why I do what I do," Camara said, "and why I must fight my government with any means possible. They are evil exploiters of the people."

She shuddered out a breath. Weren't those almost

Witt's exact words? And why Marina did what she did, as well? To stop the evil exploiters of the world from hurting innocents like Dina. From using them, subjugating them, condemning them to lives of misery and sorrow.

Like Witt, she was an idealist. She believed in doing her part to make the world a better place, so people everywhere could enjoy the same freedom and privileges she did. Naive? Perhaps. But that belief lay at the very foundation of her life.

Everything she'd read and heard said Camara was an evil exploiter, too. But he truly seemed to care about Dina and hate what had been done to her and her village. Was the intel wrong about him?

Feeling suddenly unsure of herself, she glanced at Witt, who stood propping an elbow on the massive marble fireplace mantel. His icy answering gaze jolted her. There wasn't a hint of uncertainty or sympathy in it. If he'd been affected by Dina's ordeal or Camara's speech it didn't show.

Witt turned to Camara. "What does all this have to do with us?" he asked.

For a moment she was taken aback by his coldness. She knew he cared passionately about the plight of his homeland, to the point of working against his own people to effect change and justice. Did he think Angola was somehow different? Or unimportant?

She gave herself a mental shake. No. Of course he didn't. He was just doing his job, she reminded herself. They hadn't been sent here to make judgments on Camara's motivations or character, but to find hard evidence that he was involved in savage and illegal activities. She herself had overheard him wishing Corbett Lazlo dead, a man who worked tirelessly for justice and freedom.

"We don't want anything to do with politics," Witt said.

"My God, darling," she said, careful to maintain her sympathetic expression. "The girl was raped. What can we do to help punish these bastards?" she asked Camara.

The barest smile passed through the Angolan's expression. He hesitated, flicking a glance at Witt, then back to her. "Yesterday the French boy told you about Ndinge Memebe, yes?"

She remembered. "He's the boss of another African diamond cartel, your biggest rival, who is trying to take over here in Paris." One of the many things she'd reported to Dalgliesh that morning.

Camara nodded. "Memebe works with someone high up in our government, supplying bribes to the army generals, financing the current reign of terror."

"Who?"

Camara ignored her question. "You'll recall their next shipment of rough diamonds is coming into Marseille day after tomorrow."

She did. Dalgliesh had been elated with that bit of information.

"I want you and Mr. von Kreus to meet the shipment," Camara said. "Get the diamonds for me. And kill Memebe."

For a moment she stood frozen in shock.

"That last part will cost you," Witt said into the sudden silence. He didn't seem the least bit fazed by the bloodthirsty order.

She shouldn't be, either. In an instant, all her previous sympathy for Camara evaporated.

She planted an avaricious look on her face. "You get us a good deal, baby," she said to Witt, making a split-second decision. "While I find the little girl's room, if I may?"

Camara didn't have a problem dealing only with Witt. In fact, he seemed to expect Marina to let the men handle the negotiations. Typical macho jerk.

She smiled sweetly when Camara gave her directions to the powder room, then grabbed her purse and sashayed out of the salon. Witt would keep the bastard occupied. In the meantime, she'd do a little exploring.

The scumbag belonged in jail. And it was her job to find the evidence to put him there.

Now was as good a time as any to start doing just that.

Surprisingly, Camara didn't have a lot of security in place. Marina was actually shocked at the complete lack of video cameras or motion detectors in the halls or even armed guards. Other than his two hulking bodyguards—who had both been dismissed below stairs to eat their meal—and a single sentry positioned at the front door, there was no muscle in sight. Either Camara was very stupid or he was extremely confident in his safety. She voted for the latter. His ego was big enough to believe himself unassailable in his own home.

Which in a sense was probably true, she realized. Armed African rivals were hardly likely to attack him here in France. They'd save the blood and violence for their home turf, where legal repercussions were likely to be nil. No, the biggest danger to Abayomi Camara here in Europe would be arrest by the police or one of the international security agencies. Guards, cameras and motion detectors would be useless against them. To safeguard himself from law enforcement he would need a whole different set of countermeasures—bribery, extortion, threats. She hoped she would find evidence of those on his computer, along with information on his illegal diamond business.

But first she had to find the computer. And she wouldn't have a lot of time to search.

Chances were, the computer would be in an office on one of the upper floors. After scanning the expansive hall in which the powder room was situated, she made a beeline for the grand front staircase and ran up the stairs. Debating for a moment whether to pull her Glock from her purse, she decided against it. Tough to pretend to be lost if you're aiming a gun at whoever surprised you.

Cracking open each of the heavy wooden doors leading off the central corridor, she swiftly checked all the rooms on that floor—bedrooms, sitting rooms, even a media room containing every conceivable video device known to man, other than a computer. None of the rooms appeared to be an office.

She quickly located the back staircase and continued up to the top floor, which was much smaller than the other two. There were only four doors off a square foyerlike landing. She opened one of them. An elevator.

The second door was locked. She made quick work of the lock and found behind it the master bedroom—gigantic and much more lavish than any of the others. If the computer wasn't in an office, it would be in here.

She darted a glance at her watch, again debating. No. She'd already been gone over five minutes. Better to move on.

The door across from the master bedroom opened easily. Unfortunately. Because when it did, she was greeted by the sight of Camara's two muscle-bound guards seated in front of a sleek, high-tech computer. They were laughing, bottles of beer in their hands. When the door opened, they froze and stared at her for a few seconds. Their salacious grins slowly spread across their faces, which she suddenly noticed were flushed and filmed with sweat.

What the hell had they been doing?

"Well, well," one of them said softly. "What do we have here?"

A series of sounds from the computer jolted her. Sounds of a female in the throes of orgasm. They'd been watching Internet porn.

Great.

The two men were on their feet in an instant, stalking toward her, their hooded eyes bright with an alcohol-induced glitter. Or was it something else?

"Are you lost, woman?" one said knowingly, in a deeply accented voice. He was staring at the long expanse of her legs, exposed by the miniskirt. The other one was ogling her breasts.

She started backing up, forcing a giggle. "No. Just taking a tour of the château," she said, gesturing around with her hands.

"All by yourself?" the first man asked. They were closing in on her fast. "What a shame. Such a pretty woman, to be left all alone. Where is your man?"

She subtly positioned her body to deliver a series of karate blows, should it become necessary. If these two stooges thought they could take her, they were in for the surprise of a lifetime.

"My fiancé and Mr. Camara are talking business. I wanted to see the rest of the house. It's so beautiful, I couldn't resist."

"I'll just bet you couldn't," snapped a different voice from behind her. A furious voice. *Witt's voice.*

She spun to him, wondering at the anger beneath the words. "Wh-what?"

"Yes, what?" Camara demanded of her, his gaze cold and calculating. "What are you doing up here?"

Witt strode up to her and took her arm firmly in his grip. "As I said, I apologize for my fiancée's outrageous behavior. I should have warned you to have your girl accompany her. She can't help herself." He looked Marina in the eye and scowled. "You may give it back now."

Okay. She was truly flummoxed. "G-give what back?"

His mouth thinned, as though in disgust. Then he reached up, slid his hand under the ragged collar of her T-shirt and pulled out a small object. She started at the slight tremor in his hand as he held out a gorgeous, inlaid pillbox she recognized as one that had been sitting on a table in one of the rooms on the floor below. No doubt priceless.

What the—?

She certainly hadn't stuck it in her bra. Witt must have palmed it. But why? Her eyes went from Witt's blazing blue ones to Camara's mistrustful black ones and back.

Ah.

Witt was saving her butt. Camara must have gotten suspicious of her absence. Got it.

She swallowed, and lowered her eyes abashedly. Meanwhile, Larry and Moe were backing away from her, and she noticed them surreptitiously shut off the computer. Cowards.

"I'm sorry, darling," she murmured to Witt with the slightest note of unrepentance. "You know it's not my fault. Kleptomania is a disease."

"Apologize to your host, not me."

He hauled her over to Camara, who stood frowning thunderously down at her.

"I'm truly sorry. It was appallingly rude of me." She gripped her purse in her fingers, ready to produce her gun at the least sign, and waited for his reaction.

It wasn't what she expected.

Camara laughed. A belly laugh, starting at his stomach and exploding out of his mouth in a great rolling wave of mirth. It seemed genuine. Then he took the pillbox from Witt's hand and presented it to her with a bow.

"You are perfect, Miss Bond," he said between hearty laughs. "Exactly right to work for me. Next time just ask, and I will give you any of my possessions you desire." His black eyes flashed with dark humor. "For a small price."

She shivered at that last addition, spoken with such lethal coldness. How could she ever have thought this man had a conscience? He was a viper, not to be trusted under any circumstances.

Unlike Witt.

She glanced at him with a mixture of annoyance and admiration. She could have handled the situation. She could have. But she had to admit, no matter how much it irritated her, the outcome was much better because of his quick thinking. He'd obviously seen a potential problem and prevented it by seizing control of events. In a way that actually turned the problem into an advantage.

No wonder he was so good at his job. No wonder Corbett Lazlo valued him so highly.

She was beginning to, as well.

Witt von Kreus was the kind of man she could trust with her life. Could trust to have her back. Could trust to bail her out of any situation.

Well, almost any.

Unfortunately, she wasn't particularly worried about her life or her back.

The thing she really worried about was...her heart.

Chapter 8

"But I found Camara's computer!"

Witt ground his teeth and avoided Marina's triumphant gaze. He wasn't sure he could speak rationally with her yet. He was still too furious.

After enduring an endless dinner with an overly jovial Camara, they were now driving back to Paris along dark country roads. But Witt just couldn't hold it in. Pulling the Land Rover to the side of the road, he leaped out and stood drilling his fingers through his hair in agitation.

"What the *hell* were you thinking, conducting a search of the château on your own?" he gritted out when she joined him in the outside chill. The harshness of his voice echoed through the surrounding black, silent fields. "Are you *bos*—insane? Those apes could have killed you! Or worse!"

She scoffed, looking more indulgent than worried in the bright slash of the Land Rover's headlights. "Nah. They were too fixated on my legs."

"More like what was between them," Witt said angrily. If he and Camara hadn't gone upstairs when they did…

Verdomme!

His temper hit the roof. He grasped her in a steely grip, desperately wanting to shake some sense into her. "You think I didn't see how they were leering at you when we came into that room? How they were advancing on you? Getting ready to— My God, Marina! You think government soldiers are the only ones who rape innocent women?" he practically shouted.

He must have gotten through to her, because the indulgence in her expression finally faded. Her eyes narrowed. "You really don't get it, do you?"

"Get what?" he snapped.

"That this is my job. That I am just as competent as you are. That if those gorillas had tried anything like that they'd either be dead now or wishing they were."

He stared at her, grappling with her words and the murderous look on her face. Fighting to get his ire under control so he could understand what she was trying to say.

But all he could see in his mind, all he could think about, was her lying bleeding and violated on the floor with those two grinning sacks of *shite* standing over her laughing.

For the first time since leaving his homeland, for the first time since watching his sobbing mother wave goodbye to him forever at their farm gate, for the first time since that horrible day so long ago when his boyish naiveté had been hacked from him with a dull and bloody machete, he felt close to losing it.

He swallowed hard, and swallowed again. Then dropped her arms and stalked off down the road. He halted, jammed his hands on his hips and spun back to her.

"Get in the car," he ordered. "Get in the car and drive to my flat. Wait for me there."

"But how—"

"Don't argue with me Marina! Just do it!" he growled.

Then he turned and kept walking. He needed distance. Needed his perspective back. He needed to get as far away from Marina Bond as possible.

Permanently.

He couldn't do this. Couldn't be involved with her. Couldn't be reminded what it felt like to care this deeply. To have your heart ripped out when something bad happened to those you loved. He couldn't go through that. He couldn't.

Not again.

It took him about twenty minutes marching along the verge of the road to calm down and collect himself enough to inhale deeply, lift his gaze from concentrating on the black mud and tangle of weeds under his boots so he wouldn't trip, and look around to see where he was.

It was probably around nine or ten, the night chilly but not cold. A soft breeze rustled the dry leaves of nearby trees and rattled seed pods in tall weeds growing in the ditch beside the darkened blacktop.

To his surprise, he saw he was coming up to a small village. Antique gaslights artfully illuminated quaint timbered houses that clung to the road like a jumble of puppies to their mother. Music floated out from a wine bar nestled among them. Tiny round tables dotted its front courtyard, covered by a vine-bedecked pergola dripping bunches of fat purple grapes. From the bar's open doors and windows, warm yellow light spilled over a dozen or so smiling patrons who sat sharing glasses of wine and family and camaraderie.

The sight made Witt's heart hurt. It reminded him too achingly of home. Of the things he would never have in this lifetime.

He had to turn away when he saw Marina. She was sitting alone at a table for two just outside the circle of light, watching him. She'd just figured she would disobey his orders and wait for him. The woman was impossible.

She didn't understand. Couldn't possibly understand what made him to want to—no, *need* to—protect her. She thought he was a chauvinist who didn't give her credit for brains or skill at her job. But it wasn't that at all. Not even close.

He squeezed his eyes shut, slammed his heart closed, turned back and walked over to her. There were two glasses of red wine on the table, one of which she was slowly spinning between her fingers. Jetting out a breath, he sat. And downed his wine in two gulps. He signaled the waiter to bring another.

"How did you know I'd come this way?"

She didn't raise a brow, just replied calmly, "Only one road, going in one direction. Not a big mystery."

She didn't seem to be angry at him anymore. Though he wasn't totally sure. Her expression was…guarded.

A long time went by before either of them broke the silence again.

"Who was she?" she asked quietly.

He sighed. He should have known Marina would see right through him, through his careful facade. That she would see below it all and cut to the very core of him, instinctively understanding what drove his soul and his being.

He didn't want to tell her. Didn't want to talk about his troubled past. Didn't want to be reminded of the nightmares. But she probably deserved the explanation.

"Her name was Sarah. Her father was a worker on our farm," he said, gazing out into the darkness of the French countryside but seeing a faraway place and a distant time. The most painful in his life. "I was sixteen and loved her. We'd grown up together, more or less. It was election day—whites only, of course. A group of blacks demonstrated at the polls for equal rights. That night a gang of white vigilantes went around to the farms with machetes and murdered the workers who had demonstrated. Sarah's father was one of them. They raped and killed her, too. I found them both the next morning."

He swallowed down the bile of the memory and looked up.

Marina's eyes were filled with tears. "I'm so sorry," she whispered.

"The next night, the families of the dead workers retaliated. Twelve whites were murdered, including a young girl from my school. She was also raped first."

A lone tear trailed down Marina's cheek.

"When injustice goes unchecked, everyone suffers," he murmured sadly.

They finished their wine, walked wordlessly to the car, and he drove them back to the city, wrestling the whole way with whether he should take her to his place and not let her out of his sight ever again or drop her off at her own flat, call Corbett, get a new assignment in China or Timbuktu, anywhere but here, and just get the hell away from her and all the desperate feelings she had no business dredging up from the deep, dark recesses of his heart.

He chose the second. He wasn't a coward, but he knew when he was beaten.

At least he thought he did. He made it all the way to her street. He even got as far as her building, where a gray silhouette in a yellow-curtained third-floor window was the only sign of life at this late hour. Gripping the steering wheel with white-knuckled fingers, he halted in front of the entrance, and she reached for the Land Rover's door.

To leave him.

Once again he felt the blinding pain of a last farewell.

No! a protest roared inside him.

He couldn't do it. Couldn't let her go. Before her fingers touched the metal handle, he jammed his foot on the Rover's accelerator and sped down the deserted street.

"Witt! What are you doing?"

"Taking you home."

"But you just—" He darted her a fierce scowl and her eyes widened. "But—"

"Don't say a word, Marina," he growled. "Honest to God, don't say a word."

He could practically hear the pounding of her heart as her mouth closed and she swallowed heavily. But she didn't say a word.

He took her home.

She looked scared, like a nervous little girl, all the way up the elevator. He couldn't look at her. Because suddenly he was assailed with huge doubts.

What was he doing?

This was impossible. Everything was impossible. He might want her, she might want him, but to give in to these feelings of desperate need would be lunacy. He couldn't give her a life. She couldn't give him what he truly wanted—a family of his own. To try for something like that in their situation would be pure madness. They both knew it. It would be cruel beyond words—for both of them—to pretend otherwise. And what if, God forbid, something happened to her? He couldn't live with that. Not again. The risks were too high.

So after he unlocked the door and checked his flat for disturbance, he took her hand and led her to the bedroom. There he put her in the center of the room and took a step back.

"Get some sleep," he told her, hardening his heart to the sudden look of hurt and bewilderment that seeped into her eyes. "I'll take the sofa."

With that he turned on a heel and left her standing there.

Alone.

He strode to the sofa and determinedly lay down.

Alone.

He told himself he was doing the right thing. Things were too complicated. He wasn't ready for this. A real relationship between them would never work. He could protect her, but not touch her. It was best this way. He had to close the damn case, then move on with his life and live it the way he was destined to from the start.

Alone.

Marina stood in Witt's bedroom feeling like she'd been gut shot.

He'd left. He'd left her. He'd told her he was

taking her home—*home!*—and then he'd left her standing by herself in his bedroom with her heart pinned to her sleeve like the silly, foolish, lovesick girl she obviously was.

Now what should she do?

What *could* she do?

Go out to the living room and beat the crap out of him?

She'd feel better, but hardly productive.

Go out there and fall to her knees, beg him to…to…

To what?

Hell, she didn't have a clue what she wanted from him. How could she beg for something when she didn't even know what to beg for?

Maybe just ignore him and this whole stupid mistake? Maybe then the hurt would go away.

Yeah, sure.

She closed her eyes and drew in a long, shuddering lungful of air and let it out slowly. Cleansing her mind of his image, cleansing her heart of her feelings for him. She opened her eyes, praying she'd been miraculously cured of her wayward emotions.

Her heart seized up in her chest.

He was standing there. In the doorway.

His anguished eyes met hers, and a small, desperate sound from her throat mewled through the absolute stillness of the room.

The next second his arms were around her, pulling her to him, holding her in a fierce embrace. She flung her own around his neck, clutching him close. Never wanting to let him go.

"I've changed my mind," she said, her voice splintering. "If all you can give me is sex, that's fine. I'll take it."

"Marina—"

"No, don't talk. I just want you to stay. Please don't leave me alone. Not tonight."

"I'm not going anywhere, *liefde*," he murmured, kissing her lips and her eyes and her cheeks. "I'm yours as long as you want me."

That will be forever, she wanted to tell him. But she didn't dare. Because he didn't want forever. He didn't want any more than just this.

This fleeting pleasure. Momentary comfort.

Which was okay. Because in the end neither did she. Really, she didn't. Forever was a dream neither of them could afford to indulge in. Not as things stood. And neither of them was willing to sacrifice the life they loved, the ideals they lived by, in order to make that dream come true.

Were they?

He backed her up to the bed, scattering clothes everywhere as they went, then scooped her onto the mattress and lowered his powerful frame on top of hers. He sank into her, thrust his full length into her welcoming body. She clung to him, wrapping herself around him, drawing him closer and closer and letting herself be filled by his hard flesh and his seductive scent and his fiery passion.

She let him take charge, of her body and her will. For this moment in time she was his, his to do with as he wished. His to possess. His to use for his pleasure. Because from his possession came her pleasure. And from his pleasure came her hope.

Hope for what?

For love?

No, surely not that.

No, not for love.

He touched her and kissed her, withdrawing to kiss his way down her body, to pleasure her with his mouth and tongue. She trembled on a crest of exquisite bliss, of total surrender, of aching want. And shattered in a million shards, calling his name. Refusing to think about tomorrow.

Then he filled her again and they became one once more. Sharing the same space and breathing the same air, moving with each other as two parts of the same body.

It felt different than being with a man had ever felt before. With Witt, she felt...complete. She felt... secure. She felt...like they were making love.

There was that word again. That forbidden word.

But it wasn't love.

They weren't making love.

They weren't.

Just ask Witt. He was in love with a ghost from his past, not her.

He grabbed Marina's hands and laced his fingers through hers, moving them above her head. He held her captive as he pounded into her, his breath coming like a locomotive, his thick length scything into her harder and harder, faster and faster. Bringing her higher and closer, until she was about to explode.

One, two, three more thrusts, and with a hoarse shout he shot her over the edge, into oblivion.

When Marina awoke, she expected Witt to be gone from the bed, as he'd been yesterday.

But he was still there. Spooned at her back, his arms banded around her, her head tucked securely beneath his chin.

His arousal was just sliding into her.

She smiled, but stayed still, pretending to be asleep, wondering what he would do. She was amazed he had the stamina. She wasn't sure she could move even if she wanted to. They'd made love nearly all night.

He pushed in all the way, and his arms tightened a shade. Then he sighed contentedly and stayed just like that, unmoving, except for the steady beat of his heart against her back and the gentle stir of his breath in her hair.

It felt good. Bone-deep good.

And she knew in her own heart something had changed.

During the night, somewhere between the frenzied sex and the savage need, the toe-curling satisfaction and the total surrender of self, something had changed between them.

Something amazing.

Something terrifying.

This was the real thing.

For her, anyway.

She melted back against him, savoring the feel of

his sturdy body quietly joined with hers. No urgency. No demands. No grasping for that which remained stubbornly out of reach. Just pure physical communion.

They lay like that for a long time, him adjusting every so often, giving a gentle thrust to keep himself hard inside her.

It was wonderful. She'd never been so tranquil, so at peace, in her life.

She might have dozed, except that every nerve ending was awake and alive, every sense alert to the nuance of his movement, the smell of his skin, the sound of his breath in her ear, the touch of his fingers as they slid between her thighs and slowly, gently, brought her to an achingly tender climax, which resulted in his own.

Afterward, he turned her and kissed her, deep and long. Then looked up toward the window. The first glimmer of sunlight was peeking through the curtains.

"We should probably get up," he murmured, his voice registering reluctance.

Back to reality.

"Mmm." She didn't want to move. She never wanted to move.

"I was thinking," he said. "We should sneak into Camara's château today."

Her eyes popped open and she peered up at him. "Excuse me?" Had she heard correctly?

"You know, unauthorized entry."

"Seriously?" Not that she was opposed to the idea. Just surprised he'd suggested it. And included her in the plan, if the "we" was any indication.

"Since we'll be the ones meeting Memebe's diamond shipment tomorrow, not Camara, we need to find something else to arrest him with. And now that we know where his computer is—" Witt smiled wryly, tapping her nose "—I'm guessing that's where we'll find our evidence."

Suddenly she felt all warm and fuzzy inside. She smiled back. "Do you really mean I'm invited to this party?"

His smile turned lopsided. "You're telling me I've got a choice?"

Great sex and the man could be taught, too. What more could a girl ask for?

"Nope," she said, flinging back the covers. "When do we leave?"

He stretched out on his back, hands stacked under his head, gloriously naked, delightfully rumpled, wickedly grinning. "Just as soon as you cook me breakfast, woman."

She hiked her brows. And took it as a challenge.

They didn't make it out of bed for another hour.

Or maybe it was two.

And they never did get breakfast.

Witt didn't like doing this, not one bit, but he had to choke back his fears about Marina's safety and treat her as an equal on this little incursion. More than an equal. He needed to prove to her that he *did* trust her and her abilities. That he honestly believed she was as capable as he to do this job. Which, of course, she was.

But trust and competence had never been the issue.

His reluctance had always been about his need to keep her safe and out of harm's way. Okay, so maybe he was a male chauvinist pig, but there it was. He didn't like the thought of putting his woman in danger. He liked the reality even less.

On the other hand, he'd suggested she go in today so that he'd be justified in taking the more dangerous job himself tomorrow. He definitely didn't want her meeting face-to-face with Ndinge Memebe, Camara's rival diamond kingpin. Especially not when they were supposed to kill him. Corbett Lazlo was still working out what to do about that small detail.

Witt watched Marina deftly scale the château wall and disappear over the roofline. Alone. It was the hardest thing he'd ever done in his life.

Marina had said there were no cameras nor motion sensors in the château. Only one man guarded the front door. And Camara's white limo had driven down the road toward Paris fifteen minutes ago with him and his two bodyguards onboard. As long as Marina could avoid the door sentry and any alarms, she should be fine.

He just hoped it wasn't a trap. Camara seemed to trust them—especially after Witt had exposed Marina's supposed secret, embarrassing kleptomania. But the man was far from stupid. He could easily have called in extra guards or set up new electronic surveillance and then left the château, as a test. To see if Witt and Marina really were who they said they were, or if they'd break in…just as they were doing.

Don't think about it, he ordered himself. Marina would be fine. She was a pro. She'd spot any surprises and deal with them. He had every confidence.

Nevertheless he pulled in a deep breath and said a little prayer. Any help he could get was welcome.

"You okay?" he asked in a bare whisper. They were both wearing earpieces with built-in mikes so they could communicate. If she needed help, he wanted to be able to respond immediately.

"I'm in," came the soft reply. "Bathroom window. All quiet."

Thank God. "Guards?"

A few heartbeats passed before she said, "None visible. I think we're good. Proceeding to Camara's office."

Witt tried to bite his tongue, but before he could stop himself, he said, "Check for electronic security before you go in."

"Yes, Daddy," she murmured, the eye-roll clear in her voice.

Ouch. "Wouldn't want anything bad to happen to my baby," he said softly.

She didn't reply, but somehow he knew she'd smiled at that. If reluctantly. Sometimes she could be such a hard-ass. But he knew inside she was all soft and gooey.

"The door's locked. Hold on."

More time ticked by. "Talk to me, baby," he whispered, getting nervous. She hadn't spoken in at least ten seconds. An eternity.

"Okay, I got it— Good grief. Laser sensors."

"Where?"

"Inside the office."

Bloody hell. This was new. "How bad?" He had nightmare visions of her slink-sliding into the office through a complicated laser matrix, twisting and turning like a pretzel.

"Amateur city. The guy needs a serious security upgrade."

Nevertheless he broke out in a cold sweat and kept silent. Not a good time to ruin her concentration, no matter how rinky-dink the setup. It only took one slip of the—

"Okay," she murmured. "I'm through. At the computer. Booting up. Linking."

He let out the breath he'd been holding. "Have I told you how much I hate this?" he said between his teeth.

"Daddy needs to relax. Damn. It's not even passworded."

He cursed softly. "Which means we're not going to find anything at all on the computer. We should have known. Otherwise he'd have done that security upgrade."

"Never know. Copying the hard drive now." She sounded so confident. Despite himself, his blood pressure started leveling off. Everything was going well. In five minutes she'd be out of there and—

Suddenly the scream of an alarm pierced the air.

His heart stopped dead.

She'd been caught!

Chapter 9

On the roof, a flock of birds scattered in panic at the ungodly noise made by the alarm sirens. Witt's pulse took off with them. He vaulted to his feet, ready to go in after Marina, guns blazing.

"Bollox," she swore in his earpiece.

"What's going on?" he demanded.

She cursed again. "Must have tripped one of the lasers." There was a rustle and her breath quickened. "I hear the guard coming up the stairs."

Witt drew his weapon and took off for the château. "That's it. I'm coming in."

She was sprinting, breathing hard into the mike. "No! I can make it."

He halted at the edge of the garden, in a chaos of

indecision. Wanting to give her a chance. Yet needing to protect her. "You've got five seconds."

A door closed. Another rustle. "Stay where you are," she said. "I'm out."

The whine and snap of the rappelling line drew his attention to the smooth château wall. She was zipping down it at full speed.

The mansion's front door suddenly burst open and the guard ran out onto the gravel drive. Witt dove behind a manicured topiary. Holding a machine gun in a two-fisted stance, the guard spun a circle checking for whatever had set off the alarm. In the split second before the guard spotted Marina, Witt saw her roll behind the bushy border plantings under a first-floor window.

The guard jogged clear around the mansion's outside perimeter, then made another careful circle in front of the door, his search more thorough this time, but thankfully still didn't see either of them. He stood and cocked his head, listening, for several long minutes. Witt held his breath the whole time, praying for a cat to run across the roof or something, to explain the alarm. Nothing appeared, but eventually the guard straightened, slowly lowered his weapon and went back inside.

Witt eased out his breath in relief. But neither he nor Marina moved. A few moments later the siren cut off abruptly. They stayed under cover for another five minutes before she cautiously emerged from the bushes and crouch-ran back to where he waited for her.

Wordlessly he grabbed her in a fierce hug. "That

was too close," he murmured after he'd gotten his galloping pulse under control.

She looked up at him. "Nah, piece of cake." Her eyes were alive and glowing.

"My God, you're enjoying yourself! You *like* the rush! Don't you?"

"What can I say?" She grinned unrepentantly. "But it was even better because I knew you were out here waiting to rescue me if things went wrong."

He wanted to shake her and embrace her at the same time. "You are completely mad, you know that?"

"Makes me good at my job."

He couldn't argue with that. But it didn't make him feel any better. If anything it made him feel worse. It meant she routinely pulled crazy stunts like this.

No. Not crazy. *He* had suggested this sojourn to begin with, knowing Camara's security was lax and thus the danger minimal. And Witt had to keep reminding himself that danger was part of her job. A big part. His, too. If they were going to make this work between them he'd have to wrap his head around that and accept it.

The question was, could he, even if he wanted to make it work?

He thought of Sarah and his heart hurt.

"Let's get the hell out of here," he muttered.

Now was not the time to be making any kind of decision about the future. Not with the buzz of adrenaline from the job rushing through his veins; not when just last night he'd resolved to sever their connection completely, only to change his mind seconds later and promise her he'd stay as long as she wanted him.

Yerre, he was messed up.

What was it about this woman that had his whole world crashing and burning? That made him question firm decisions made long ago? That had his mind paralyzed with indecision and his tongue making promises he couldn't possibly keep?

He had a sinking feeling he knew the answer. And it wasn't good.

"The embassy!"

Witt shook his head for the third time. "Not gonna happen, *skat.*" Marina could protest until next year, but no way was SIS seeing the contents of Camara's hard drive before he did. "We're going to the Lazlo Group first. We'll send Dalgliesh a copy from there." After Witt and Corbett had a look first.

Marina's jaw clamped. "This is *my* operation, von Kreus. *I* get to call the shots."

He sympathized. He did. But he wasn't prepared to budge on this issue. For her own good. Aside from everything else, there was that bug in her mobile to consider. Until they nailed down what that was all about, whether Camara had a mole in SIS to worry about, Witt wasn't taking any chances.

"No," he simply said, and pointed the Land Rover toward La Défense. She should feel privileged that Corbett trusted her enough to let her into the heavily guarded, top-secret Lazlo Group headquarters.

"I'm sorry," he said when she sent him a mute glower.

She'd see he was right. Eventually.

Lazlo HQ was situated in the area of Paris known as La Défense, a clump of tall, modern buildings that housed much of the French financial district and many multi-national corporations. The Lazlo Group offices were on the ninth floor of a staid, non-descript gray building. There Corbett maintained a posh but fairly standard private investigations firm through which much of their legitimate, low-profile business was run. But that was just a front. The real workings were in an underground complex deep below the building, accessible only through a rigorous obstacle course of security checks. Corbett actually owned the property, so he'd had it built to his personal specifications during the initial construction.

It was quite a spectacular place, if you were into high tech. Witt had always gotten a kick out of the spy-thriller atmosphere, even if at times it seemed a bit over-the-top.

After leaving the Land Rover in the building's underground car park, he took Marina to a door marked in French, Emergency Exit—Authorized Personnel Only. Using his personal code, he opened it and held the door for her, directing her into a tiny room that resembled a steel-walled vault. The door closed after them with a reverberating thud, effectively locking them inside what Lazlo employees affectionately called the Box.

Witt placed his palm on a glass panel in the wall. Most people would think it detected his palm print or fingerprints, but in fact it was picking up a signal from a tiny microchip implanted in his hand—the latest thing in security technology. A thick steel panel above it slid open on a state-of-the-art optical scanner. He stepped up to the screen, eyes wide open; it scanned his irises and instantly beeped its approval.

"Your turn," he told her.

"Me?" She looked at it warily.

"There are sensors in the floor that determine the number of people standing in the Box. The doors won't open again until every person has been cleared."

She hesitated. "But I've never been here before. It doesn't have my iris scan on record."

He chuckled. "No."

She frowned, then peered into the scanner. It beeped. Her brows went up to her scalp. "Damn. I'm not even going to ask."

He grinned. "Best not to." A large panel on the far wall slid back to reveal an open elevator. He swept a hand toward it. "After you."

The steel doors whooshed closed behind them. "Good afternoon, Mr. Von Kreus, Ms. Bond," a pleasant female voice said from nowhere.

Marina inspected the inside of the elevator suspiciously, trying to spot the cameras and speakers. Witt knew she'd never find them. He'd tried for years.

"Welcome to the Lazlo Group," the voice continued in cultured tones. "Mr. Lazlo is waiting for you in the computer lab. May I take you there now?"

"Yes, thank you, Mademoiselle Nord."

The official Lazlo receptionist was beautiful, cool and elegant, but Witt would not want to go up against her in a fight. Of any kind. Part of the job requirement was a black belt—she had three—a marksman weapons rating and Special Forces assassin training—from which she'd graduated top of her class.

"Be sure to pick up Ms. Bond's swipe card as you exit," Mlle. Nord said.

"We will."

The elevator moved silently downward and came to an almost imperceptible stop; the doors opened automatically. Witt grabbed a small plastic card from one of the two armed guards who stood to either side and greeted him with smiles as he and Marina walked out into a long, brightly lit tunnel.

"We'll need to see your ID," they said to her. "And to check that thumb drive you're carrying in your pocket."

She shot him a glance. Yeah, they'd been subjected to a weapons/electronics scan in the elevator, too. Absolutely nothing entered the complex that the guards didn't know about and approve.

"My gun?" she asked, holding out her jacket to reveal her shoulder holster.

"Nope," the guard replied matter-of-factly. "We know you carry a Glock 23C with a full load of 40 caliber Smith & Wessons plus a spare cartridge on your belt. Don't worry, the boss vouches for you."

"Ho-kay, then."

When she was cleared and the thumb drive plugged in, inspected and returned, Witt handed her a plastic swipe card. "You'll need this."

At the end of the tunnel was another glass panel along with a scanner. He repeated the same procedure as before, except instead of scanning his eyes, this one scanned his ear. Different sections of the complex had different biometric security. That prevented terrorists from kidnapping an agent and simply cutting off one body part to gain access. They'd need the whole person with them, alive, to even have a chance. Comforting, in a perverse sort of way.

"Place the card over the glass," he told Marina when it was her turn. "Say your name, then show the scanner your left ear."

She did so. "You are *not* telling me your computers have my ear scan on file."

He chuckled. "They do now."

"Good grief," she said as they exited the tunnel into the sleek, gleaming main complex and turned down a hallway toward the computer lab. "And they say SIS is paranoid."

"It keeps our agents safe," he said. He used to think the security measures were excessive. Not anymore. "At least, we hope we're safe. Corbett is hoping we'll find some leads on Camara's hard drive as to who is behind the vendetta against the Lazlo Group."

"Well, I still don't know why you insisted on coming here first." She darted him a frown. "Wait, surely you're not thinking SIS is somehow involved in this vendetta?"

Sharp as a tack, that woman. That was exactly what worried him and the boss. "Corbett doesn't like to think so, but it's not outside the realm of possibility. He has a long history with SIS, you know. Not always friendly. And until we figure out who is threatening our agents…"

"My dad mentioned Corbett worked for SIS— MI6—a long time ago. Didn't they fire him?"

"Essentially. As a fairly new agent he was wrongly accused of badly botching a case—they called it treason, actually—but he was subsequently cleared. But by that time the damage had been done. There may still be some old grudges hovering around in the dark corners of Vauxhall Cross."

"Once accused, and all that."

"It's possible."

She shook her head. "Ridiculous nonsense."

"Anyway, you can see why he's anxious to check over Camara's files first. That way we're sure we're seeing everything uncensored."

"I understand," she said.

And he really thought she did. Her loyalties seemed to lie more on the personal level, aligned with real honor and justice rather than to some particular brand of law enforcement alphabet soup.

"But there's another reason for caution," he added. "Abayomi Camara is the client of a British attorney named Barrett Jenkins. There is a tentative connection between Jenkins and someone we believe works for SIS. We have no actual proof of this mole, and we're hoping our suspicions are unfounded, but better to be safe than sorry, as they say."

She gazed at him skeptically. "You really believe the British intelligence service has been comprom-ised by Camara? That he has a mole working for him inside?"

Witt shrugged. "The Lazlo Group has been con-ducting an investigation into it. So far there's only circumstantial evidence, but we're still digging."

"My God. I was hoping you'd say I got it all wrong."

"Unfortunately, not likely," he murmured.

She stopped walking and stared at him. Hard. Considering. "Witt, what aren't you telling me?"

Taken by surprise, he stared back, mouth parted. "Why would you say that?"

She pursed her lips unhappily. "You *are* hiding something from me."

Damn, he'd walked right into that one. *Eish,* he couldn't *believe* he'd fallen for the oldest trick in the book. He really had to tell her about the bug he'd found in her phone. But he needed Corbett's go-ahead first.

Meanwhile, he made a dismissive gesture. "Marina, I'm a secret agent. I have lots of secrets. Even from you."

She just gave him a look.

They walked the last few steps to the computer lab and he waved his hand over the scanner next to the door. He tipped his head up, this time to allow a video camera to scan his facial features and compare them to his file picture. The door buzzed and he went in to wait for Marina to complete the security procedure.

But Corbett waylaid him and took him aside as soon as he entered. "We need to talk."

The boss didn't look happy. "What's up?"

"That bug in Marina's phone."

"Yeah?"

"We traced it to a specific section inside SIS."

Witt let out an oath. "I knew it. Which one?"

"The GCHQ liaison section. De-encryption."

"The guys who work with SIGINT? The code breakers? Damn it to hell, Corbett, we've got to tell her—"

Corbett shook his head to cut off the discussion. Marina was walking up to them.

"Hello, Mr. Lazlo. It's been a long time."

The boss took her hands in his. "Please, you're all grown-up now. Call me Corbett. So good to see you again, Marina." He smiled and kissed her on each cheek in the traditional continental greeting.

Witt had to tamp down a sudden spike of jealousy. Lazlo had at least a good ten years on him, but was still a good-looking man, in a stern and conservative sort of way. A woman could do a hell of a lot worse.

Witt gave himself a mental kick. Okay, not good. *Jealous?* Of Corbett? He really had to keep a lid on the ol' hormones.

He pulled out the thumb drive onto which Marina had copied Camara's hard drive and moved the conversation back to business. "Let's see what Lucia can find on this for us."

Lucia Cordez was head of the Lazlo Group Information Technology department. She knew everything there was to know about computers and their mysterious workings. A pure whiz. She was also gorgeous, sexy, and had an obvious soft spot for Corbett. Witt kept hoping the boss would notice her. He had the distinct impression so did she. But that would be out of character for their old-fashioned lone-wolf employer.

When they got to Lucia's work station, Witt met her friendly gaze with a question in his eye, but she just sent him a wry look and a lifted shoulder. Ah, well. One of these days the old man would realize what he could be enjoying.

Corbett gave her the thumb drive. "Work your magic, Lucia," he said.

Witt noticed Marina had her arms crossed and was determinedly studying the impressive array of computer equipment—and avoiding looking at him. Almost like she was…jealous, too. Of Lucia? He wanted to laugh out loud. Instead he moved close to Marina, pretending to look over her shoulder as Lucia stuck the drive into a USB slot and started to work the keyboard like a Steinway.

He casually put his hand on Marina's bottom.

She kicked his shin.

This time he couldn't stop a grin. She *was* jealous! Thank God he wasn't the only foolish one.

He sobered immediately when a deluge of

numbers and files began to flash across Lucia's computer monitor. She clicked a key, and the images transferred to a big LCD monitor mounted on a wall to one side. With another click, the files organized themselves into several neat groups on the screen.

"Looks like we've got correspondence, financial info, personnel files, business records, photographs, and—" she snickered "—Internet porn."

Corbett cleared his throat. "I think we can skip the porn for now. Can you run a word search on *Lazlo* and see what pops up?"

"Sure thing." Lucia's fingers flew on the keyboard. The search came up empty.

"Damn. Try *Corbett*."

Same result. They tried a few other permutations, and still came up with nothing.

"Sorry, boss. No files on the vendetta," Lucia said somberly. "At least nothing obvious. I'll comb through all the files individually, but that'll take time."

"Put in *SIS*," Marina said quietly.

Lucia nodded, and typed in the abbreviation. When nothing came up, she tried *British Intelligence* and *MI6*. Again nothing appeared.

"Try just *6*," Marina suggested. The nickname a lot of old-school agents used for MI6, or SIS.

Instantly several hundred files popped up. After eliminating the obvious financial ones, a few dozen were left. It took them all of about five seconds to read down the list and arrive at the same one. In unison, they said, "There!"

It was a file called "6contacts."

Lucia double-clicked the icon and it opened. It was a list of initials and phone numbers. At the top of the list was BJ. Under that was JW.

So much for having their fears proved wrong.

Witt and Corbett gave each other a grim look and said at the same time, "Barrett Jenkins and Jared Williams."

Marina blinked at them in disbelief, then stared at the familiar initials on the list. "That can't be right. I've worked with Jared Williams!" She turned to Witt, then Corbett. She didn't like the looks on their faces. Suddenly it hit her. "You knew about this before today, didn't you?"

"We actually had him arrested last month," Witt admitted.

"I didn't hear anything about that."

"The PM kept it quiet. The investigation is ongoing."

"What was he arrested for?"

Witt pushed out a breath. "Illegal surveillance and breaching national security."

Anger swept through her as her trust shattered completely. "Damn it, Witt! You knew about this and didn't tell me?"

"There was nothing to tell, Marina. We had no idea his activities had anything to do with your operation."

"And even if we did, Agent von Kreus couldn't have told you," Corbett cut in. "That information is top secret. He was following strict orders."

"That is such bollox!" she spat out. Turning on a toe, she stalked to the door. She had to get out of there before she did something rash. But she was stopped by the security measures. Hard to make a really good exit if you had to swipe a card and have your facial features scanned first.

Naturally, Witt caught up with her. She gritted her teeth.

"*Skat,* please. You know our business is a house of cards at best. I was as honest with you as I could be."

"Sorry, that's not good enough. I went out of my way to help your organization, disobeyed *my* strict orders, and this is what I get for my loyalty? Screw you, von Kreus." She turned away.

"Marina, don't. Don't make this personal."

She spun back, fury making her sputter. "Oh, I don't intend to. Not anymore. You want business? I'll give you business. From now on, you—" she emphasized the word with a jab of her finger to his chest "—are *just business.*"

The door buzzed, she swung it open so it smacked against the wall and stormed out.

"Wait, Marina! There's more," he called to her.

Bloody hell. She should have known.

She halted in place, tapped her foot a couple of times in frustration, then turned to him. "What?"

"I… There's a transmitter. In your mobile. Someone's bugging you."

Her attention snapped to her purse, which held her phone. "A bug," she said past her clenched jaw. "And you didn't see fit to tell me that, either."

She had reached the stage of surrealism, feeling

so betrayed that she went into a blank zone. She could no longer feel anything.

"It's my fault," Corbett said briskly, coming over to join them. "Witt wanted to tell you. I wouldn't let him. I didn't want whoever is listening to your conversations to suspect you're on to them. That would have been far more dangerous than not telling you. I knew Witt would be with you for protection. And I know you're good enough at what you do not to compromise yourself."

She narrowed her eyes at the two of them. "You do, eh? More orders, Witt?" she asked, drilling him with an accusing glare.

His eyes narrowed right back at her. They flashed angrily, filled with blue fire like the beautiful opals of his homeland.

He stepped into her space and glowered down at her. "Don't even go there, *skat*," he growled.

"Marina," Corbett said crisply, "You've worked for SIS long enough to know that double-blinds and need-to-know are routine operating procedure. You cannot let your emotions affect your performance or your judgment in this job. If that happens, you are utterly useless as an agent."

His reprimand stung. But it did the trick. She took a big mental step back.

She was acting like a ninny. There was no place for hurt feelings or recriminations in this job.

She closed her eyes and took a deep breath. When she opened them, she nodded. "You're right, of course. I was totally out of line."

There was also no place for personal relationships.

This situation with Witt could not go on a day longer. They'd gotten too close, too deep, too fast. There was no way she could keep her feelings for him objective or compartmentalized from the job when everything was as intertwined as it was on this case.

She had to choose.

It was either Witt or her job. She couldn't keep both.

One of them had to go.

And it had to be now.

Chapter 10

"You people need to see this."

Lucia Cordez's sharp tone drew everyone's attention away from the tense situation at the door and back to Camara's files.

"What is it, Lucia?" Corbett asked with a frown, striding over to her workstation.

Marina wanted nothing more than to get the hell out of there and never return. But that was not possible. She had a mission to complete. An important one—a career maker or breaker. And this was unfortunately a joint operation. She had to stick it out for the duration.

Not a problem. She was stronger than the situation. She could do this.

She hoped.

The sooner she closed the case, the sooner she could get away from Witt and get on with her life.

Because with a sinking heart she understood that leaving him was the only choice she could make. They might be on the same side philosophically, but their loyalties were to different organizations. What had just happened proved that hurt and betrayal was the inevitable outcome. The only way a relationship would work was if one of them quit or changed loyalties. Witt wasn't interested in forever. And she wasn't about to give up the job she loved for anything less.

Lucia spun toward them in her swivel chair. "The files on Jared Williams and Barrett Jenkins are bad. Really bad." With a click she sent the documents to the big screen on the wall and laid them out for all to see.

Witt and Corbett whistled.

"Looks like Williams won't be getting out of jail anytime soon," Corbett said.

"And this is enough to put Jenkins away for life," Witt added.

Marina stood in shock. The files contained the precise details of a long history of what appeared to be bribery or payoffs: dates, amounts and account numbers. Combined, over a million euros had changed hands.

"This is too incredible," Marina said, not wanting to believe it. "Why would they do it?" she whispered. Not that there was any doubt. A million euros was a lot of money. But the human misery caused by the blood-diamond trade… Willfully allowing it to continue went against everything Britain and America stood for. Everything she and SIS worked to achieve. All betrayed for greed. It disgusted her.

"Lucia," Corbett said, "please send a copy of these records to the British prime minister right away. He'll see that Jenkins and Williams are dealt with appropriately."

Marina roused herself. "Meanwhile, our job here is to make sure Camara and his dirty business is shut down for good."

Witt nodded. "With luck we'll get enough hard evidence for his arrest in Marseilles tomorrow, when we meet Ndinge Memebe's shipment coming in from Angola."

Memebe, whom they were supposed to kill.

"I'd be willing to bet Camara himself shows up," she ventured, "after the bullets stop flying. To see for himself that we fulfilled our part of the deal."

"You don't think he trusts us to top the bastard?"

"You're kidding, right?" She blinked. And started at his impassive expression. "You're not really planning to kill Memebe, are you?"

He smiled humorlessly. "Of course not. Personally, I vote for giving Camara the double cross he's expecting."

She gave a shaky grin. She hadn't believed Witt would do it. Not really. "Camara won't like that. No telling what he might say in the heat of our betrayal. One of us should wear a wire."

"That can be arranged," Corbett interjected. "When are you two leaving for Marseilles?"

"I reserved seats for us on the fast train first thing in the morning," Witt said. "Memebe's ship is due to dock sometime around noon."

"Good," Corbett said. "That gives us the rest of today to come up with a detailed plan and decide what kind of backup you'll need so I can round up the manpower."

"No," Marina protested. "I should coordinate backup with SIS." But even as she said it, she winced.

"Under the circumstances," Witt said, "maybe it's best not to bother SIS with this particular part of the operation."

She grimaced. "My section chief's initials weren't on Camara's list. Besides, if Dalgliesh were corrupt, why would he have initiated an international investigation of Camara in the first place? Maybe he even suspected someone in SIS of being dirty, and this was how he hoped to prove or disprove his suspicions."

"Very likely," Corbett said diplomatically. "But until we know for sure, you should keep all information about your movements tomorrow between these four walls. And you should also leave your mobile phone here. We can send it on a little trip with a decoy in the morning."

She stifled a quick spike of anger at the reminder of *that* betrayal, and gave a short nod. "Right."

See? She could play nice.

But something must have shown in her face, because Corbett said, "Two more of our agents were killed yesterday, Marina. In Turkey. I don't want to have to bury you, too. Remember that when you question the reason behind my orders."

When put like that, it was impossible to stay angry with him. He'd always had her back. Hell, he'd stepped in and saved her life when her own father hadn't been able to. There were not a lot of people one could trust in this business, but she knew she could trust Corbett Lazlo absolutely to have her best interest at heart.

Witt, on the other hand, was another story. She might trust him with her life—and she did, despite their differing professional loyalties—but she knew very well his interests did not include her heart.

But she wasn't going to think about that.

There were more important things going on now than her own pathetic love life.

It took most of the afternoon to work out their strategy for dealing with Ndinge Memebe and the Marseilles shipment of illegal blood diamonds, hammer out how they could get Camara to incriminate himself if he showed up and then to secure the high-level French permissions required to run an armed operation on their soil.

It was dinnertime before Marina had a spare moment to think about dealing with her own emotional train wreck.

"Where would you like to have dinner tonight?" Witt asked, slipping on his jacket as she grabbed her purse to leave.

The two of them had spent hours working closely with each other, concentrating on the important task at hand without letting a single personal word or look pass between them. Now, suddenly, all the storminess from earlier tore loose from where she'd carefully banked it at the very back of her mind, threatening to pour in a deluge all over her.

"I'm pretty tired," she said, striving for a casual, neutral air as they went through the many security checks to get out of Lazlo headquarters. "Think I'll just have an early night of it."

She was proud of how calm and unemotional she managed to sound, while inside she wanted to scream at Witt at the top of her lungs to just leave her the bloody hell alone. As long as he didn't look at her or touch her, she'd be fine. She hoped.

"I'm all for turning in early," he said, following her through the long tunnel that led to the car park. "But we should eat first. We'll need all our strength for tomorrow."

"I'll find something at home," she said, and kept walking.

She made it as far as passing through the final checkpoint at the exit door before his hand shot out, slapping onto the solid steel doorframe to prevent her from going any farther. His expression was icy. "What are you trying to say, Marina?"

At least he wasn't touching her. She sucked it up, standing as tall as she could…though annoyingly, her chin didn't even reach his collar.

"I'm trying to say good-night, Witt. I'll see you

at the train station in the morning." She ducked under his arm to walk up and find the Métro. The tunnel door closed behind them both with a dull clang.

"Like hell," he growled, grabbing her hand. "You're not leaving my sight until this thing is done and Camara is behind bars."

"Witt, you can't—" She cut off the words and counted to ten. Trying to be composed. And reasonable. Despite the sudden electricity flying between them where their skin touched.

Inside, a battle raged. She didn't *want* to be reasonable. The man was messing with her mind. Her body. Her heart. Hell, her whole damned life. Suddenly the things she'd always deemed important had started to seem less so. To seem inadequate. Like she was settling for second best.

Which was insane, because what she did *was* important. It was vital to the peace and stability of the whole world. Jobs didn't *get* more important than that.

And yet…somehow when she was with Witt, it all felt…not enough.

Which made her even more insane.

She wanted to launch herself at him and pound his chest with her fists until the desolation was beaten out of her and he understood what he had done to her and her previously work-driven life. To her previously uninvolved emotions. To her previously unbroken heart. She wanted to shake him until he understood all that. And then to go away. Permanently.

Instead, she gazed up at him unflinchingly. "Witt. This thing with us isn't working and you know it."

A muscle in his cheek ticked. As if he were trying to keep his own floodgates tightly closed. "Yes, I know."

"You betrayed my trust. I'm mad as hell at you."

"I know."

"We both need some distance. Badly."

"I know."

"We both need some *sleep*."

"I know."

Her frustration flared at his unhappy agreement with everything she said. "I don't want to get involved with you! You don't want to get involved with me, either. You said as much last night when you tried to stay away from me."

"I know."

She could tell he wanted to look away, but he didn't. If anything, his stare intensified. She wanted to smack him.

But that wouldn't be very professional behavior, so instead she said what she figured was on his mind. "The problem is, we can't be in the same room together without tearing off each other's clothes."

The muscle ticked again. "*Yessus,* Marina, I know all that." This through clenched teeth.

She was hanging on by a thread. "We can't stay together tonight, Witt! I can't deal with this case and you, too. It's too hard."

But rather than letting her go, he took hold of her other hand and pulled her to him, looking down at her with a turbulent expression.

He worked his jaw. "I'm sorry things have gotten

so complicated, *skat*. I know you don't think a whole lot of me right now, and I don't blame you. But if you imagine for a single minute I'll leave you alone tonight, you don't know jack about me."

She opened her mouth to retort and he scowled warningly.

"And before you say a word," he said, cutting her off, "it has nothing to do with your competence. It has to do with me, and my need to protect you. Okay, so I'm a Neanderthal, I'll admit it. But I need to know you're safe from Camara and his goons. I've seen what men like them can do to a woman, and no way am I—" He swallowed down the words. "You are coming with me tonight. It's not open for discussion. You can come willingly or we can do it the hard way. Your choice."

Part of her wanted to seethe with fury at his audacity. She really did. But the rest of her was caught in the memory of his face as he'd told her about his first love, who had died at the hands of violent madmen.

With anyone else she might have taken his very chauvinistic, very male, very proprietary edict as an unconscious—if a bit dysfunctional—declaration of love. With Witt, she knew better. He was a man who did his job well and thoroughly. She was part of his job. His protectiveness was because of guilt over the past, not worry over the future.

"Fine," she said.

She didn't want to fight. Didn't want to talk about it. Didn't even want to think about why that bothered her so much. It wouldn't serve any purpose other than to confuse and upset her.

"Fine?" he asked.

"You win. Let's just get out of here. Please."

Witt was a bit surprised at Marina's quick acceptance of his somewhat tyrannical orders. But glad. He took it as a good sign. Maybe she'd forgiven him.

"But don't think for a single minute," she said, throwing his words back at him as they walked toward the Land Rover, "that we'll be sharing a bed."

Okay, maybe not.

Not that he planned on letting a trifling detail like forgiveness stop him. Spend the night under the same roof without her in his arms? Not bloody likely.

"Whatever you say, *skat,*" he replied.

He wasn't worried. They'd been dancing to this same tune for three nights now, and the sun had always risen with him inside her. Tonight would be no—

Suddenly a loud bang detonated around them. Pain exploded like a glittering bastard in his shoulder.

"Down!" he shouted, ignoring the excruciating pain and spinning to shove Marina behind the closest car. But she'd already rolled clear, had her Glock drawn and was returning fire.

Yessus. Was he getting slow in his old age?

He pulled his gun and tried to aim. It was the strangest thing. His hand shook and he couldn't get a proper grip on it. His finger jerked and his head went woozy and he couldn't figure out where the hell the shots were coming from. The next thing he heard was the clatter of his weapon on the concrete floor.

In fact, that was the *last* thing he heard. Then he was swallowed up by a vast, dark, cottonlike silence.

Witt burst into consciousness in a rainbow of pain. Two medics were wheeling him up to a private, unmarked ambulance he dimly recognized as one of the Lazlo Group's. His body was being jostled; it felt like someone was kicking and grinding boot heels with spurs into his shoulder.

"Hey!" He muttered a few choice suggestions and swear words before he realized one of the EMTs was a woman, and that Marina was hovering over the other one, holding an IV bag and peering down at him. "Sorry," he croaked contritely. His mother would be so disappointed.

"Shut it, von Kreus," Marina ordered crossly. "Let the people do their jobs."

His mother would like her, he decided, suddenly feeling much better. He smiled. Or tried to smile. His face felt numb. Drugs? What was in that IV, anyway? And why did he need it?

He tried to frown. "What the hell happened to me?"

"What the hell do you *think* happened?" she snapped. "You were shot."

Shot? Beauty. Not.

A memory—if somewhat vague—of what had happened sifted through him. How long had he been unconscious? Not long. Marina's gun was still drawn and her eyes darted around the car park, though he could plainly see they were surrounded by a swarm of Lazlo security officers and agents, including Corbett who was currently shouting into a mobile phone.

Witt did his best to concentrate on Marina's face as he was loaded into the ambulance. No easy feat. Wait. Her face and coat were smeared with scarlet. Alarm jolted through him, temporarily lifting the cobwebs. "You're hurt! Bleeding!"

"It's your blood. He was aiming at you, Witt."

"Yeah, sure he was," he muttered, wincing as the EMT stuck another huge needle into his arm. "Because it's my phone that's bugged and my organization that's riddled with traitors."

Marina climbed in behind them and buckled into a jump seat. Her eyes latched on to his. "I caught a glimpse of him. It was the same guy who shot at us at the hotel. And the Arc de Triomphe. I'm sure of it. And *you're* the only one he's hit."

God, he hated it when he was wrong. "Maybe he's a really bad shot," Witt muttered wearily.

"Maybe," she said. The siren started to wail and the ambulance took off. "Where are you taking him?" he heard her ask the attending EMT. But a wash of drugs rushed through his mind, muddying his thoughts too much to follow the answer. He hated that, too—not being in control of his own mind.

But Marina would protect him.

He reached for her hand. "Stay with me," he whispered. And passed out.

* * *

Okay, this was not good.

Three hours later Marina sat nervously by Witt's hospital bed still holding his hand. There was nothing to worry about, she assured herself. He had come through surgery just fine—the wound was clean and the bullet had missed anything even remotely important as it passed through his shoulder—and he was awake, but still all drugged up. Corbett had insisted on a heavy sedative, and she agreed, because they both knew if Witt were allowed his complete faculties he'd insist on checking out of the hospital and continuing with the mission tomorrow as if he'd never been shot.

Shot. Good Lord. *Again.*

Obviously someone out there had it in for Witt in the worst way. Part of the vendetta?

"Gottabeamistake," Witt said, slurring the words together into one long one. "He *must* be after you."

He was insisting on having this conversation even though he was barely conscious. The man was stubborn as a mule.

"I'm telling you, being hit twice isn't a coincidence," she said. "He may be a lousy shot, but he was aiming at you, Witt. Accept it."

He let out a sigh. "Gottagetthebastardthen," he slurred. "Too much to livefornow." He gave her a loopy smile.

She smiled back, her heart squeezing. If only he meant it. But it was the drugs talking. He'd been saying mushy stuff like that since coming out of the anesthesia.

He patted the bed awkwardly with their joined hands. "Come 'ere. Wannafeel yourbody nexttome."

Just the drugs.

"I don't think the doctor would approve."

"Screw the doctor." He slid a few inches closer to her. "Actually, gottabetteridea…" He managed an exaggerated wink.

She chuckled. "I'll bet you do."

His face fell to serious. "How'dheknow where I was?" he asked.

"The doctor?" It was hard to follow Witt's line of thought when there was no logic guiding it.

"Shooter. Mustbepartof the vendetta," he said with a sage nod. Duh! "But how'd he know I was at the hotel?"

She regarded him. They'd talked about this briefly before, but hadn't reached any conclusions. Of course, she hadn't had all the pertinent information then.

She resisted grinding her jaw. She was over it. She was.

"My phone had a tracking device in it," she reminded him tersely.

"Makes no sense," he replied, "to follow you, but shoot me."

He had a point there. "Then they must have found out some way. Who did you tell where you were going?" she asked. They'd been over this, too.

"No one."

"Come on. No one?" He had to be forgetting some small but important detail.

"Corbett phoned me at the last minute, after he'd

gotten on the plane that morning. You'd just called him with the location of the meet. I went straight there."

She thought about that. There was only one conclusion possible. "Your phone must have a tracker in it, too."

His head wagged back and forth. "Nope. I check mine every morning. Plus Corbett had a comprehensive check run on all Lazlo phones, equipment and spaces. Nothing."

"The shooter must have been tailing you, then."

Witt actually looked offended. "That amateur? I'm insulted."

"That amateur managed to shoot you twice," she said dryly.

"I was distracted," he muttered, casting an accusing eye her way. But it was a soft glare, filled with tender— if unsteady—meaning. "After I met you, maybe," he said in prickly tones. "But trust me, no one was following me *before* our meeting." He wagged a swooping finger at her. "So, it must have been *your* bug that led him to us. Therefore, it was *you* he was shooting at." His expression was muzzy but triumphant.

Unfortunately, she could find nothing wrong with that bit of logic. The problem was the theory didn't fit the evidence.

She shook her head. "You said my phone was bugged, not tracked. But I'll grant you it may have been my mobile that led the shooter to the hotel. But if you were the target, it really makes no sense… there was no way he could possibly know it was you who'd show up at the meeting. Even I didn't know that. I was expecting Corbett."

They gazed at each other for several heartbeats, trying to puzzle it out. All at once it hit her.

Oh, my God.

Corbett!

Witt must have come to the same realization at exactly the same moment. His eyes widened, mirroring her own. He let out a curse.

"The shooter thought you were Corbett!" she exclaimed. "*He's* been the target all along!"

"But I look nothing like Corbett! How could he possibly mix us up?"

"Maybe…" She thought desperately. "Maybe he doesn't know what Corbett looks like?"

Witt blinked at her several times, obviously trying to wrap his drug-dampened mind around that idea. "He's trying to kill a man and he doesn't even know what he looks like? A stretch, Marina."

"Yes, but what other explanation is there that fits the evidence? We've eliminated every other possibility. And our shooter does seem to be quite the amateur assassin."

"My God. You're right." With woozy urgency, Witt reached for the tubes and leads stuck into his body with one hand and his mobile phone with the other. "Gotta-warn-Corbett."

She jumped up and threw herself at his hand grappling with the IV tubes. "Witt, stop! You're in no shape to do anything. I'll call him." She grabbed the phone from him. "Just lie back and be good."

"But—"

"Don't make me shoot you again," she warned. "What's Corbett's speed dial?"

"Three," he said. "And six. And nine." When she hiked a brow, he lifted his good shoulder, winced and said, "Increases the odds of hitting the right one in an emergency."

Smart. She punched six. When Corbett answered, she told him of their theory.

He was silent for a few moments. Then, "It sounds crazy, but it fits. Good work, you two."

Witt wiggled his fingers at her. "Let me talk to him."

"Witt wants to talk to you," she told Corbett. "Don't even think about letting him come along on the op tomorrow. Not in his condition."

Corbett chuckled. "If I know that man, you better tell the doctor to put him in a straitjacket."

"Don't think I won't," she muttered, and handed Witt the mobile.

"It's just a scratch," Witt said to Corbett with a grimace. "Don't listen to her."

Corbett did all the talking, punctuated only by Witt's occasional grunt or hum, so she had no idea what was being agreed upon. It made her very nervous. And irritated. She didn't trust either of them to put Witt's health first.

"You've been shot," she said sternly when he hung up and she was none the wiser as to their plans. "You can't leave the hospital until the doctor says it's okay."

He gave her a remarkably steady look for a man

strung out on drugs and pain medication. "I know," he said. Which made her even more nervous and irritated.

They were up to something. Definitely.

She tried to remember if she had her handcuffs with her. She eyed the tubular metal bed frame. It could hold him. For about a nanosecond.

"I'll be very unhappy if you do something stupid," she ground out.

He smiled and patted the bed next to him again, suddenly looking tired. "Better make sure I don't, then. Keep me company while I sleep."

She knew what he was doing. Trying to prevent her from going home alone. Not that she had any intention of leaving him for a minute. It made a lot of sense that Corbett was the target, but she wasn't taking any chances.

She was as trapped as he was. Might as well be comfortable. Well, semicomfortable. Ignoring the empty bed on the other side of the room, she climbed onto the narrow strip of mattress next to his good side, minding the tubes and wires. He flipped the thin blanket over both of them with a contented sigh.

"Thank you," he murmured, and pulled her close. "I wouldn't have been able to sleep if you'd left."

"Because you're afraid I'll do the mission tomorrow on my own?" she murmured, nestling close to his solid warmth. Barely covered by a flimsy hospital gown, his muscular body was familiar, impressive and tempting. She had to remind herself he was a wounded man and to keep her hands to herself.

"Yeah. Afraid," he mumbled, his voice fading to

almost nothing and his breaths deepening. He whispered something else, which she strained to make out.

She froze in disbelief. She couldn't hear his words. Not quite.

But they had sounded very much like, "Because I love you."

Chapter 11

Marina strode briskly out of the Marseilles train station and glanced around for the Lazlo agent who was supposed to meet her there. As planned yesterday with Witt and Corbett, a red car zipped up to the curb in front of her. It was one of those cute Smart Cars that looked like a miniature loaf of bread cut in half.

The driver leaned out. "Ms. Bond?"

She nodded, noticing he was wearing an earpiece. As she opened the car door, she looked over her shoulder, half expecting Witt to walk up behind her talking into a similar gadget, with one of those annoyingly smug smiles of his.

He didn't.

She wasn't sure whether she was relieved or disappointed.

No. Relieved, definitely. The last thing she wanted was to see Witt face-to-face in the cold light of day. If she did, she might blurt out something she'd truly regret. Like asking him if he'd really meant what he said last night.

Of course he hadn't. It was the drugs. If he'd even said it at all. She couldn't be sure. The words had been spoken in barely a whisper.

No. She had to put it out of her mind.

She'd been relieved that he hadn't awoken when she'd slipped out of his hospital room at the crack of dawn this morning. And yet… It had been almost too easy to escape. Which made her suspicious—her natural state, especially when dealing with Agent von Kreus. It wasn't like him to give up and let her go alone on this op without at least throwing a fit. Maybe he'd still been sedated….

The driver of the red car, who introduced himself as Paul, passed her a small duffel bag as he pulled into traffic. It contained an array of goodies Corbett had promised her for the mission.

She plucked out a small-caliber Beretta, which she tucked into her waistband to back up her Glock; a throwing knife in an ankle holster, which she strapped on under the leg of her jeans; a mobile camera phone, which she stuck in her back pocket and four microtracking devices, which all went into the tiny change pocket in the front of her jeans. The T-shirt she wore was too tight to hide anything.

"The mobile phone has a GPS locator," Paul explained, swinging the car toward the shipping docks. "If you have to switch off the phone, the locator powers on automatically after fifteen minutes."

"Handy," she said.

"The four microtrackers will activate after five hours. That should give you plenty of time to plant them and get away."

They were to be used if she ran across anything that might lead deeper into the cartel's European network by tracking its physical movements. Like the bags of rough diamonds. Even though she and Witt had been hired by Camara to intercept them, she was pretty sure Camara himself would show up after the meeting to claim his new property. She'd hand over the diamonds, trackers in place, and then Lazlo agents could follow them down the line.

She also could swallow one of them if things got really crazy.

Which it easily could. The main wild card in her day was the Ndinge Memebe "assassination." That would take some finessing.

"What about the special bullets Corbett said would be here?" she asked Paul.

He ducked his head at the duffel. "In an ammo box."

The Lazlo Group had invented a kind of tranq-dart-cum-paintball bullet that knocked out the target and made it look like he was bleeding without actually injuring him. She dug around and found the box.

She pulled out one of the bullets. "Looks exactly like the genuine article."

"That's the idea. The fake blood is not terribly realistic," he said, "but it should fool anyone watching long enough for your man to hit the ground."

"And the drug works quickly?"

"It absorbs instantly through the skin. He'll collapse within seconds. Just aim for thin clothing."

She popped out the clip from her Glock and replaced the top two bullets with the tranqs. Two shots should be enough. She didn't want the real bullets to be too many pulls of the trigger away.

As she worked, Paul spoke a few rapid words of French and turned onto a seedy harborside street jammed with squalid warehouses.

"Who's on the other end of that thing?" she asked, jerking her chin at his earpiece.

"Lazlo," he said, pulling the vehicle to the side of the road. "The boss wanted to run this one personally." He pointed down the block to one of the shabby structures. "That's the meeting location. You won't see them, but three of our agents have been in place for a couple of hours." He checked his watch. "Memebe and his men aren't due to arrive for another thirty minutes."

"Any sign of Camara?"

"Not yet."

"Okay, let's get to where we're supposed to be."

The plan was for Lazlo agents to grab Memebe's French contact person, whose place she was taking, just before he reached the meeting, and she'd use him as leverage with Memebe. The other Lazlo agents were positioned inside the warehouse in case things went pear-shape. Her butt was as covered as it would ever get.

Corbett definitely took care of his people. Quite a contrast from what she was used to at SIS. There, she was usually tossed into the middle of things on her own, sink or swim. Not that she'd ever been on an op quite this dangerous before…. Those were reserved for the big boys. She was usually relegated to what they called "undercover surveillance," her role nearly always being glorified temp work…as she was doing at Glace Chaude. Which was why she'd resented it so much when Witt horned in on the mission just as things were getting interesting.

But she had to admit his presence had really turned up the heat on the case. Hell, on all fronts. If nothing else, life was never boring around Witt, she thought philosophically.

To her annoyance, she realized she missed him. Not just personally but professionally. She *liked* working with him.

Bollox. When had that happened?

Paul tucked the tiny car into the mouth of a narrow alleyway a few doors down from the warehouse. This was where the ambush would take place. His earpiece squawked softly.

"Memebe's arriving early," he told her after listening a moment. "He's approaching the warehouse."

Sure enough, a minute later a long, black limo rolled past and drove up to a large bay door that a bodyguard jumped out to unlock and raise. The limo disappeared inside.

"He only brought two guards," Paul added after another exchange.

Marina let out a measured breath. "Excellent. So far so good. Now we just have to nab the contact man and we're golden."

Luckily, Etienne the snitch had told them the name of the guy and they'd run a background on him, so there was no guesswork involved.

Except that when the lone car finally rolled down the street at the appointed time, the driver was not the man they expected.

It was the manager of Glace Chaude. Monsieur Henri.

Before Marina could stop them, the Lazlo agents swiftly and efficiently detained Henri and convinced the would-be smuggler to surrender.

She swore a silent oath. Bloody hell. How had she and Witt not known about Henri's double dealings? Was this his first attempt at doing more than simply selling the diamonds? Or had he been doing it all along?

Okay. This could still work. In fact, it could work to her advantage. This way *she* wouldn't have to be the one double-crossing Camara. She could play hero to Henri's traitor and get the evidence to convict not only Camara but Henri, as well. And be much safer while doing it.

Witt would be proud of her.

"Duct tape," she said to Paul. "Got any?"

"Glove box."

She found the roll and jumped out of the car, striding up to Henri. "Tsk, tsk, tsk. Going behind Camara's back, Henri? Not healthy."

"What the hell…?" The arrogant manager's face registered shock as he recognized her, one of his meek little shopgirls, as being part of his kidnapping. She loved it when people finally realized they'd underestimated her.

"You are in a lot of trouble, *mon ami,*" she told him matter-of-factly, tossing the duct tape up and down on her palm.

"I don't know what you're talking about," he sputtered. The agents had bound his wrists behind him with those plastic cable handcuffs that looked like garbage bag closers. He jerked at them but, judging by the grimace of pain on his face, he only succeeded in making them tighter. "Release me at once!"

"Don't think so. Here's what is going to happen." She tore a strip of duct tape off the roll. "You and I are going to that meeting with Memebe. But you aren't saying a word." She illustrated her point by sealing Henri's mouth shut with the tape. She smiled at his muffled outrage. The man had been a real jerk to work for. Payback was sweet.

Damn, she was really starting to enjoy playing bad cop…er, girl.

She drew her Glock and casually continued, "I'm going to drag you in there at gunpoint. Then I'm going to shoot Memebe and take his diamonds." She paused while that sank in. Henri's eyes widened. So much for meek little shopgirl.

She waved the Glock in his face. "If his goons are smart, they won't try to stop me. I suggest you act scared, Henri. Very scared." She tapped his chest with the muzzle of her gun. "Because if you don't, I just might shoot you, too." She smiled again and tipped her head. "Of course, you may want me to go ahead and kill you, because when Camara finds out you've been double-crossing him, he might not be so nice."

Henri was sweating now, and his eyes looked like dinner plates. Wide, with a sheen of terror. He tried to say something under the tape. She shrugged. "Sorry, not my decision. Okay, *mon ami,* let's go." She stuck the Glock into his neck and prodded him to start walking toward the warehouse entrance.

"Aren't you forgetting something?" a deep, masculine voice said behind her.

She didn't have to turn to know who it was. But she did anyway, her heart leaping at the sound.

"Witt!"

A thousand emotions washed through Marina when she saw her man standing there, bigger than life and ornery as a junkyard dog. Surprise—though not really—joy, relief. Then worry. What was he *doing?* The man was gravely wounded.

"Damn it, Witt! You can't be here," she said firmly. "You're supposed to be in bed."

He didn't make one of his usual suggestive comebacks. He didn't even smile. But one slightly raised brow was enough to send heat to her cheeks. She hated that he could do that to her. And loved it. God, he confused her.

"You didn't seriously think I'd let you face Memebe and his gang alone?" he said evenly, stepping closer. "I'd have to be dead. And even then I'm not so sure."

The impact of his words went straight to her heart. Her lips parted and she almost gave in. Then her gaze dropped to his bandaged shoulder and the sling that held his left arm tight across his chest, and she remembered.

"Witt, you're in no physical shape to do this. Or mental. Either the drugs you're on or the pain you're in will impair your concentration and decision making. It's too dangerous."

"I'll leave all the decisions to you," he said. "I'm strictly backup on this gig. But I *will* be with you in there." His tone held no possibility for compromise. "Either by your side or at your back, but I'm going in."

Unfortunately, she knew he meant it. She blew out an irritated breath. "Has anyone ever told you what a royal pain in the ass you are?"

The shadow of a smile passed his lips. "What do you think?"

Oh, that was easy. She'd never met anyone so frustrating, so overbearing, so bossy, so arrogant or so…wonderful…in her whole life.

She sighed. "I think if we're going to do this, we'd better get to it."

* * *

The plan went off without a hitch.

Right up until the part where Camara showed up. That's when all hell broke loose.

Marina and Witt stormed the warehouse with their hostage in tow and weapons drawn. Memebe had not been expecting trouble and was easily overpowered. But he was still reluctant to hand over the diamonds. So Marina simply pulled the trigger and shot him—with the tranq bullet, of course, as planned. His two bodyguards scrambled for cover and in the ensuing chaos one of the Lazlo agents hit Memebe with a real squib, so the blood pouring from his chest looked genuine. With their leader "dead," the guards soon surrendered and handed over the briefcase containing the bags of rough diamonds.

Like clockwork so far.

Adrenaline sang through Marina's veins as she made one of the nervous guards open the briefcase so she could check the diamonds. No booby traps. Good. The stones looked drab and unremarkable, just as they were supposed to in their unpolished state. As she inspected the gems, she surreptitiously fastened a micro transmitter onto the fabric inside each of the three bags.

"Excellent," she said, snapping the briefcase closed. "From now on, you're—"

"I'll take that," Camara interrupted from the bay door. He marched into the warehouse followed by a fan of five bodyguards, including Claude from the jewelry store, and Mfana and Deco from Etienne's interrogation. Camara did a double take at Witt's bound-up arm, halting next to him. "What happened to you, my brother?"

Marina should have noted the shade of sarcasm at the last word. But she was too busy feeling satisfied with herself over predicting his moves.

Witt shrugged with his good shoulder. "Someone seems to be holding a grudge."

"Not a very good shot," Camara observed, his melodic accent making the words sound sympathetic, but Marina finally twigged to his eyes. They were flinty and cold. Uh-oh.

She straightened, instantly alert. Too late. By the time she whipped out her Glock, Camara's goons had already surrounded Witt. Three guns were pointing at his head and two at hers.

Bollox.

Witt carefully raised his hands and Claude slid the SIG from his fingers.

"What's going on here?" she asked Camara angrily. "We did what you wanted. Is this how you reward your people?"

"My people?" He chuckled, but it was not a pleasant sound. "Miss Bond, you truly disappoint me."

She still held her gun, and she knew the three hidden Lazlo agents had theirs trained on Camara and his men, as well. But they were outnumbered four to five. Four to six if Camara was armed. If the shooting started, either Witt or herself was dead. She needed to even the odds before making a move. But she had orders to take Camara alive, not to kill him. This would be tricky.

"*I* disappoint you? Why's that?" she asked, feigning outrage while playing for time. Looking for her opportunity. "I killed Memebe for you. What more do you want?"

Camara flicked his gaze to the man lying on the floor in a puddle of blood, and pursed his lips. "He certainly looks dead. But somehow I don't think so." His eyes pinned hers. "I doubt very much your superior at MI6 has given you license to kill. Has he, Agent Bond?"

The stunned silence in the warehouse was sudden and complete.

Okay, this was bad. Had Camara been aware she was an agent the whole time?

Every eye in the place darted to her. Only Witt's face registered alarm. The rest looked…pitiless.

She snorted. "You've been watching too many movies, Camara. You don't believe Memebe's dead? Check his pulse."

Camara smiled. And jerked his head at Claude to do just that. But not before pulling a Smith & Wesson automatic from under his jacket and jamming it into Witt's temple.

Marina felt herself go cold and still inside. Her gaze met Witt's and he gave a slight nod. Then everything happened so fast she didn't have time to think, just react.

The instant Claude bent over to check Memebe, Witt drove his good elbow into Camara's stomach and dove for the floor. The Lazlo agents opened up and the guards went down in a spray of crimson. Camara's S&W swung wild and Marina fired. He folded like an accordion, a shocked look on his face and blood blooming on his chest.

And then it was all over.

Marina's ears rang in the sudden cottony stillness of the cavernous warehouse. So many guns going off at once was murder on the ears. She ran over to Witt, but he waved her off.

"I'm fine," he shouted, and pointed. "Get their weapons."

The Lazlo agents appeared from nowhere to help gather guns and check pulses. One of them spoke into his earpiece, giving a crisp report to someone on the other end.

"Tell Corbett to send an ambulance," she called, pressing her fingers into the side of Camara's neck. There was the barest flutter of a pulse. "I think he's still alive."

Or maybe it was her own galloping heartbeat she felt in the tips of her fingers.

Witt joined her on the other side of Camara's body, grimacing as he knelt. A stain of red was rapidly spreading across the stark white of his shoulder bandage.

"You're hurt!" she said.

"I think I pulled out my stitches when I rolled on the floor. I'll be okay." He peered down at Camara. "But this one isn't going to make it."

"I had no choice. He was going to kill you," she

said, blinking back sudden tears. She'd never killed anyone before. Never even shot anyone. He was a bad guy, but still...

"You had no choice, *skat*. It was you or him," Witt said. His jaw tightened. "He knew who you work for. It's proof he had someone working inside SIS."

She swallowed. As much as she didn't want to believe it, the evidence was pretty strong. "Yeah," she said.

"And whoever it is, he's not going to be happy about his income being cut off when Camara dies or goes to jail."

"That's a safe bet."

Just then Corbett and Paul came running into the warehouse, followed shortly by the scream of ambulance sirens and the arrival of the EMTs. She and Witt backed off and watched as they rushed Camara onto a gurney and wheeled him out.

Then Witt turned to her. "With both Camara and Memebe out of commission, a lot of people are not going to be happy." He grasped her hand and regarded her seriously. "Marina, you need to get out of SIS. Resign. It'll be too dangerous for you to stay there."

At first she didn't understand what he meant. Then shock slammed into her. "You think the mole will try and hurt me?"

"It's not such a stretch to think someone will want revenge on you for killing Camara, putting Memebe behind bars and effectively cutting off the entire European illegal diamond supply. A lot of people will lose a lot of money because of your actions."

"B-but…but," she stammered, not even knowing where to begin. "That's nuts. How will they know it was me?"

"Camara knows. Chances are, so will his partners. Certainly the mole knows. I don't want you hurt, Marina. You've got to promise me you'll resign."

She didn't want to get hurt, either. But quitting her job was a bit drastic. "Witt, I wasn't the only officer working on this case."

"But you were the one who brought down Camara and Memebe."

Again he had a point.

Chaos reigned in the warehouse while everyone was quickly dispatched either to the hospital, the morgue or to Corbett's private jet where the agents' debriefings would take place on the way back to Paris.

Naturally, Witt refused to go to the hospital. Marina wanted to think it was because of his usual macho stubbornness, but the way he kept his good arm protectively around her and his eyes always roving for danger told her otherwise. He was really afraid for her life.

She didn't know what to think. Or to do.

Except…yeah, she did.

Damn it, this was her job! If she started running scared every time she closed a case and put away the bad guy, she'd be ineffectual as an agent. She wouldn't have to quit the Service. They'd fire her.

And another thing. She noticed that although Witt wanted her to quit SIS, he wasn't offering her any alternative.

Yeah, she noticed *that,* all right.

And she tried really hard not to let it bother her, either.

But it did.

After they got back to Paris and she'd given her report to Corbett and her statement to the French authorities, and she got the order from Section Chief Dalgliesh to catch the next plane back to London for her debriefing at Vauxhall Cross, she knew exactly what she had to do.

A clean break from Witt. That's what was needed. Otherwise their affair could drag on and on, going nowhere and doing nothing except slowly break her heart.

He'd warned her from the beginning. For him it was just sex. His past precluded anything else.

She'd tried to make that work. But she'd fallen in love with him. And though more was impossible, sex just wasn't enough.

No, she needed a clean break.

So as he was leaving to go back to the clinic to have his stitches repaired, she told him she was going back to her apartment to pack a bag.

Which was true. Could she help it if he assumed it was so she could come stay with him?

She didn't have the courage to tell him the truth. If she did, he'd just insist on going with her to London. And that would only prolong the inevitable. The tears. The heartbreak.

May as well get on with it. Put it behind her.

And simply pray she'd get over him.

Someday.

Chapter 12

"Marina?"

Gun drawn, Witt listened, then slid through the partially open front door to her apartment, the lock of which he'd just picked.

Breaking and entering without orders. What next? He was acting like a stalker. But he was desperate. And armed and ready to kill if he had to. Something had happened to Marina. He was sure of it.

When he'd dialed the mobile phone Paul had given her at the warehouse, a recording came on saying it was no longer in service. And her bugged SIS phone had also been disconnected. She wasn't at the Lazlo Group headquarters, nor was she at the hospital, nor at Witt's flat where he'd expected her to be.

She'd disappeared.

Corbett insisted she'd gone back to London. Witt didn't believe him. She would never have left him like this. Not without at least saying goodbye. Never.

He did his best to ignore the niggling voice in his head that taunted, *Or would she...?*

No! Not when he had finally made up his mind about her, about their future. About how much he wanted her despite the problems they'd have to face to be together. The fact was, he didn't think he could bear a life without her in it, no matter how big the problems. If they loved each other, they could solve anything. Together.

"Marina, damn it! Answer me!" He slammed the door behind him, wincing at the pain zinging through his shoulder.

He opened his mouth to call out again, then snapped it shut. She wasn't answering, anyway. And yelling wasn't making him feel any better.

He didn't know what he was more afraid of, that he'd find her lying dead on the floor, or that she really had left him.

No, he knew the answer to that, but both were unacceptable. He needed a third option. Like maybe she was still packing to move in with him. Yeah, that would work.

He moved swiftly through the small apartment with growing agitation. There was nothing there. Nothing but furniture. He burst into her bedroom and moved in a circle, taking in at a glance the utter absence of personal items. Not that she'd had a lot of stuff. She'd only lived there a month, a temporary arrangement while working her op in Paris. But what she'd had was gone.

Totally gone.

There was also no blood anywhere. Nothing in disarray to indicate foul play. Nothing left to *be* in disarray.

He let out a harsh oath. And another. Then he stalked out to the kitchen, picked up a wooden chair and bashed it into the floor over and over and over, until he'd smashed it into a million tiny splinters of wood.

Childish, yes. But *that* made him feel better.

For about two seconds.

How *dare* she leave without word one? Why had she left at all? She'd forgiven him about not being up-front with her. Or had she?

Doubts assailed him again.

No. Yes. Hell, she had to have forgiven him. She loved him! True, she'd never actually said so, but she didn't need to. He knew she did. It was there in her eyes when she looked at him. At least, when she wasn't furious with him about some stupid thing he'd done.

Why would she leave if she loved him?

Maybe someone really had taken her. Maybe something bad *had* happened to her, just as he feared. Whoever it was could have taken her and all her stuff, too, to make it appear as though she'd left on her own.

He had to get to the bottom of this.

He whipped out his mobile and called the Lazlo

Group dispatcher to connect him with Marina's section chief at SIS in London. If James Dalgliesh hadn't heard from her—or claimed he hadn't—they'd both know she was in real trouble.

When the section chief answered, he paused at Witt's worried questioning. Yes, Marina was here in London, he answered. In fact she was sitting across from him in his office right now. She was fine. Not in any trouble.

For a second Witt couldn't breathe. First from relief. Then from the implications.

So that was how it was. He fought to keep his cool as anger swept through him. Not in trouble, hey? She didn't have a clue what real trouble was. He'd show her trouble, all right.

"May I speak with Marina, please?" he calmly asked. Proud that he didn't yell. Didn't even raise his voice. See? He could be civilized.

There was a muted exchange, then Dalgliesh came back on the line. "We're rather in the middle of something at the moment. Can't this wait?"

That's it.

"No, it bloody well *can't* wait!" Witt barked, all semblance of composure falling to the wayside. He wanted nothing more than to reach through the phone line and strangle the pompous wanker until he understood what was at stake.

He waited impatiently through more muted words.

"Agent von Kreus?" came Marina's cool, collected voice over the line, finally. "How nice to hear from you so soon. Is there a problem?"

"Agent von Kreus?" he echoed stonily. He actually had to count to ten not to lose it completely. Make that twenty. Twice. It didn't help. *"Agent von Kreus?"* he yelled. "What the bloody *hell* is going on, Marina? What are you doing in London? I thought you were going to leave that job and move in with me?"

All at once he was thunderstruck. And understood. How stupid he was! His anger evaporated and he felt almost giddy with relief. "That's what you're doing now, isn't it!" he exclaimed. "Telling Dalgliesh you quit."

She didn't answer.

"Right?"

There was another heartbeat of silence. Then, "Um, not exactly. But now isn't really the time to discuss this issue."

This issue?

Witt's fury returned in an instant, fire hot and drowning deep.

He'd been reduced to an *issue?* Their affair, their relationship, their future, was an *issue?*

So much for her loving him.

"Oh?" he managed. Barely. "And when *would* be a good time? Although, since your precipitous departure from Paris left me twisting in the wind like a fool, I assume you're not really interested in discussing this *issue* at all."

"That's not fair," she protested, but oh so calmly. "I'm in an important meeting with my section chief at the moment. We can talk when I'm done, okay?"

"No, it's not okay!" he snapped, feeling more petulant than he had since he was two years old.

"Witt, I have to go now."

"How can I get hold of you? You don't even have a damned phone! Marina? *Marina!*"

But the line was dead. She'd hung up.

She'd bloody hung up on him.

He stopped pacing and took a deep, steadying breath. What to do. Kill her? Or kiss her to within an inch of her life, until she saw things his way?

Those seemed like the only choices open.

And guess what. To do either, he had to be in London.

All right, then. London it was.

Using Corbett's private jet, getting across the channel took less than an hour.

The evening was miserable as only a London evening can be. Cold, rainy, damp, dark. Witt looked through the taxi window at the depressing drizzle and thought the weather couldn't reflect his mood more perfectly.

What the hell was he doing here?

It didn't matter how much he'd made up his mind to try for something permanent between them. Because Marina didn't want him. On the trip over he'd come to that more-than-obvious conclusion. She'd left Paris, left him, without a word, and on the phone today had talked to him as if he were a stranger.

He'd been delusional when he'd thought she loved

him. He should just leave well enough alone, turn right around and go home.

Too bad he couldn't.

He needed to see her. Needed to look into her eyes and hear the words from her own lips that she didn't want to be with him. That she'd sooner choose her dangerous job over a life with him. A life, he realized with a sinking heart, he would probably never get a chance at, no matter how desperate he was to try.

He slumped down in his seat and sighed.

"Why the long face, mon?" the taxi driver asked, tossing his dreadlocks over his shoulder. It was rush hour and traffic was at a dead halt. "Looks like you've lost your best mate."

Witt gave a snort. "Something like that."

"Ah, I see." The driver nodded sagely. "Trouble wit your woman."

His woman. That was a laugh. "Not my woman."

"She turn you down, mon?" When Witt raised his brows, he clarified, "When you ask her to marry you?" Traffic started to inch forward.

"What? *Yerre,* no." Witt squirmed a little in his seat, reading the name on the taxi driver's license. Sam Barlow, official busybody. "I didn't exactly propose."

"Ah, I see." The driver—Sam—nodded again. "Wot then, exactly? You ask her to move in wit you?"

Witt turned back to the window, watching the storefronts roll past. "Yeah. To move in."

Although…

Now that he thought about it, he hadn't really

asked her to move in, either. He'd just assumed that's what would happen. He told her to quit her job and she said she'd pack. They'd seemed to be in agreement. What was there to discuss?

He frowned and looked up. Sam Barlow was watching him in the rearview mirror with a broad grin. "Forget to ask that, too? What *did* you ask her, mon?"

Witt scowled. He was getting very tired of this conversation. "Nothing. She knows what I want."

"Ah, yes. Because women, dey are such good mind readers," Sam said with a jovial, don't-worry-be-happy laugh. Witt's fists itched to belt the guy.

"Just drive," he growled.

Sam shrugged, started whistling to a tune on the radio and drove without further comment.

But the damage had been done. That niggling little voice had started talking in Witt's head again.

No. She had to know how he felt about her, what he wanted. She had to! Just because he hadn't gotten down on bended knee…

Yessus. Was that the reason she'd left? Because he hadn't come out and *asked* her outright to stay? How insanely ridiculous would that be?

Which was exactly what worried him. Women could be so—

Ah, hell.

When they finally reached the distinctive SIS ziggurat at Vauxhall Cross he leaped out of the taxi, dashed inside and impatiently endured the strict security checks before hurrying up to Dalgliesh's office on the fourth floor.

"I'm sorry, I'm afraid she left awhile ago."

"Where did she go?" Witt demanded impatiently.

Dalgliesh hesitated, until Witt reminded him of his Lazlo Group credentials. They always opened doors and melted walls, and this time was no different. "Upstairs. Deputy Director Roland Milleflora wanted to see her."

Witt frowned. "Milleflora?" Where had he heard that name before?

Dalgliesh nodded. "He was very unhappy about Abayomi Camara's death. He'd given explicit orders to keep him alive, to interrogate. Miss Bond will have to answer for that."

"So she didn't quit?" Witt asked, momentarily distracted.

Dalgliesh looked surprised. "Quit? She'll be extremely lucky if she's not asked to resign, but no, she didn't do so on her own."

There. He had his answer. She'd chosen her job over him.

But was it a fair choice? Since he hadn't asked her…

"Where can I find this Milleflora's office?"

Dalgliesh gave him directions, and watched from his door as Witt strode out and made a beeline for the lift.

He was going to have this out with her one way or another.

When he arrived at the correct office, he came to a sudden stop at the sign on the door which said "Roland Milleflora, Deputy Director General, SIS." Suddenly Witt remembered where he'd heard the name before. Corbett had mentioned he'd worked with the man when they were discussing possible suspects for Camara's mole. Uneasiness swept through Witt as he hurried into the office.

Marina wasn't there. Neither was Milleflora.

"They left together about, oh—" the DDG's secretary consulted the wall clock "—twenty minutes ago."

Witt's internal alarm went off in spades. "Together?"

The secretary's thin mouth turned down disapprovingly. "Quite cozy, they were, too. She had her arm through his."

Witt's anxiety increased exponentially. Dalgliesh had said Milleflora was about to fire her. Now they were all chummy?

He didn't think so.

"Do you know where they went?" he demanded.

"Afraid not." The secretary turned away and fussed with something on his desk, effectively dismissing him.

Something was definitely not right here. Witt grabbed his mobile, but before he had a chance to dial out, it rang. It was Corbett.

"Good news," Corbett said. "We found where Camara kept his records. And his business computer. Hit the jackpot."

Witt stifled the impulse to brush aside Corbett's news. "What did you learn?" he asked hurriedly, already heading out the door.

"We now know who the other mole at SIS is. An MI6 team is en route to arrest him at Vauxhall Cross as we speak."

Witt's head spun, dizzy with relief. Or was it terror? He grabbed a wall for balance. "I'm there now. I can make sure he doesn't get away in the meantime. Who is it?"

He could practically hear Corbett shake his head. "You are not going to believe this. I'm having a hard time myself."

"Try me," he said impatiently. As long as Marina was out of danger he didn't care who the hell it was.

"It's the Deputy Director General of SIS, Roland Milleflora."

Shock and horror slammed into Witt's chest like a double shotgun blast as his worst fears were realized. "Please God, boss," he pleaded hoarsely, "tell me you're joking."

"Trust me, I wish I were." He could hear the puzzlement in Corbett's voice. "Witt? What's wrong with you?"

"Milleflora. Oh, my God, Corbett. He's got Marina."

"You can't think for a minute you're going to get away with this," Marina said evenly. Well, as evenly as she could, considering she could die any second.

Not the scenario she'd envisioned for the evening—as depressing as her day had been thus far. But it was just getting worse and worse.

A deputy director general of SIS. Who'd have thought someone that high up could be a traitor? The greedy bastard.

"On the contrary. I've gotten away with it for

years," Milleflora said with haughty confidence. "I've got millions stashed away offshore, and I've had all the time in the world to plan for this eventuality. You are merely a pesky fly in the ointment. They'll never catch me."

Then it was up to the pesky fly to stop him, wasn't it?

"You can't do anything to stop me," he added arrogantly. "Just remember, a hostage is useful, but I don't *need* you. I only brought you along in case I need a bargaining chip. I'll kill you in a heartbeat if you make trouble."

"Then you better shoot me now," she retorted, possibly tempting fate. But she had to find out what he was up to.

He smiled at her. A conceited, superior smile. "Nice try, Miss Bond. But please keep in mind I've *taught* the training classes you so recently passed. You're a babe in the woods against the big bad wolf. You won't provoke me into making a mistake, so just give up now and save us both the irritation."

Hokay, then.

She flopped back in the cream leather passenger seat of Milleflora's vintage Jaguar XKE-12 and crossed her arms over her chest. "You're the one who bugged my phone, aren't you," she muttered.

"Ah. I thought you might have found that. Nevertheless it served its purpose. The minute it went off-grid I knew the game was up."

"You had to know mounting an op against Abayomi Camara meant the game was up anyway."

The corner of his lip curled down, but he didn't comment.

"Why okay the mission at all?" she pressed.

Milleflora gave her a condescending glance. "Dalgliésh would have gotten even more suspicious of me if I'd objected. Bugging his operatives in the field bought me the time I needed to get my affairs in order."

"So you could leave."

"I'm growing tired of your chatter, girl."

She was quiet for a while, then asked, "Where are you taking me?"

"Good God!" he exclaimed in annoyance. "You are a pushy little thing. Must I put a gag on you?"

"Knock yourself out," she muttered.

He reached inside his jacket and pulled out something that looked like a pocketknife. He pressed a button on one end and four inches of steel shot out the other. A switchblade.

Before she could react, he stabbed it into the flesh of her thigh. Then pulled it out again.

Pain and blood blossomed swift and hot in equal measures. She swallowed a shocked scream and let out a string of curses instead. She grabbed the wound to make it stop bleeding, battling to stifle a deluge of panic. Wow, this guy was seriously twisted.

"Next time it'll be a lot worse," he warned impassively.

"Okay, I get it," she said through gritted teeth, fighting to stay calm.

She'd thought his selling out to Camara had to do with diamonds and greed. But maybe Milleflora was a sociopath who longed for the good old days when, like Camara in Angola, MI6 was a law unto themselves in Britain, doing anything they wanted to in the name of queen and country.

A cold-blooded killer who missed his work. Not a pretty thought. Greed was far easier.

She shut up.

And thought of Witt. And how she'd left Paris like a coward without letting him know how she really felt about him.

And tried to figure out how the hell she could stay alive long enough to have a second chance.

Every law enforcement agency in Great Britain was looking for Marina and her captor. There was nothing Witt could do that wasn't already being done. He knew that. And yet he felt an urgent need to *do* something, *anything,* to find her.

It looked bad. Roland Milleflora was a real piece of work. He hadn't made it to second in command of Britain's most elite spy organization by being a diplomat. He'd earned his position through a lifetime of action in the field. Ruthless, vicious, unremorseful action. He had the reputation of relentlessly getting things done—any way he had to.

Not good for Marina.

Even Corbett looked worried. He'd jetted to London from Paris immediately upon hearing Witt's troubled explanation, bringing along a dozen Lazlo Group operatives who were all currently doing what they did best, whatever it was. Witt was the Group's lead interrogator, but there was no one to interrogate—no one M16 would let him near, at any rate. They were already interviewing Milleflora's entire staff and anyone who'd had anything to do with him for the past five years, including Jared Williams. Witt hadn't been invited to participate. So he was cooling his heels in a visitor's chair, from which he could watch and listen for breaking developments, going crazy thinking about what could be happening to the woman he loved while he sat and did nothing.

"You okay?" Corbett asked, striding past on his way from one meeting to another.

Witt sprang to his feet, gripping his aching shoulder. The pain meds had worn off and he'd left the bottle back in Paris. "Feeling totally helpless, boss. Please, give me something to do."

Corbett halted and regarded him sympathetically. "As soon as we locate any of Camara's or Memebe's missing crews, you're our man," he said. "Meanwhile—"

"Meanwhile I'm going nuts. I have to move. To do something."

"Give me a suggestion. If we had a clue where Milleflora was headed, I'd send you to intercept. But we don't."

"There has to be—"

"Excuse me," a young man interrupted politely. The kid was impeccably dressed, his hair trimmed in a trendy cut. He was holding a briefcase in his hand. The one Witt and Marina had taken off

Memebe that morning. Had it only been this morning? It seemed like a hundred years ago to Witt. The kid hefted the briefcase. "Section Chief Dalgliesh wants you to know he's sending the diamonds your people seized down to the basement to be locked in the vault. Apparently there is some kind of tracking device in them that's been activated. It's setting off alarms all over the fourth floor."

Corbett waved his hand. "No problem. The trackers are automatically activated after five hours. You're welcome to remove the transmitters from the bags if you like. They're not needed now, anyway, since the diamonds aren't going anywhere."

Witt had forgotten about the trackers. Apparently, so had everyone else. But at the reminder, his entire body suddenly froze in place. He stared at the briefcase as his mind was flooded by a single blinding thought.

"Corbett," he said. "Corbett!" Something in his tone, the urgency, or the excitement, made both the other men turn to him.

"Tell me."

"The transmitters. This morning. How many were there?"

Corbett's brow creased. "There are three bags, so three transmitters."

"No. This morning. How many trackers did Paul actually give to Marina, before we went in?"

Two seconds later Corbett's eyes widened. He said a strange word. The boss was Hungarian, but in all the years Witt had known him, he'd never heard Corbett speak the language. Until now. Witt assumed it wasn't a nice word. Before it had passed Corbett's lips he had his mobile out and was waiting for head-quarters in Paris to pick up.

"The Camara operation in Marseilles," he clipped out to whomever answered. "The tracking devices. How many were issued?"

For several long seconds his eyes held Witt's as they waited breathlessly for the answer. When it came, a triumphant smile sprang to Corbett's lips. "Find that fourth signal *now* and patch it through to von Kreus's Blackberry."

But Witt was already running.

They'd found her.

He'd be in time to save her! He would. He had to be.

And when he had her safe in his arms again, one thing was for damned certain. He was never, ever, letting her out of his sight again. Not for as long as they both should live.

Marina's leg had started to throb mercilessly. The stab wound had stopped bleeding awhile back, but the blood had dried in a thick layer, gluing her skin to the fabric of her jeans, pulling painfully every time she moved. Nice.

They were heading west. The names of the villages they passed on the tiny country lanes Mil-leflora was sticking to had a million letters and were unrecognizable as words. Welsh. She figured he was making a break for the remote coast of Wales. No doubt there was a boat tied up in some deserted smuggler's cove waiting to take him out into international waters, where perhaps a hired yacht was already speeding toward a rendezvous point to pick him up. He didn't seem in the least worried.

But then, why should he be? They'd changed vehicles three times since leaving London, and though they'd seen more police cars along the way than usual, none of them had paid the slightest heed to them. Milleflora had laid his groundwork well. But then, he'd been a master spy for over forty years, so that was hardly surprising.

What was surprising was that she was still alive.

They were approaching the sea. Marina could smell it in the brine-scented breeze. Not much longer now. But for what?

She was dying—okay, bad choice of words—to know what fate he had in mind for her. Sort of. Though she'd just as soon skip the part where she died for real, if that was the plan.

Mostly because of Witt. She'd die never seeing him again. The thought was enough to bring tears to her eyes.

Next to her, Milleflora snorted. "Are you *crying?* Spies don't cry! Good Lord," he muttered. "And you call yourself an agent. The whole bloody game is going to hell." He shot her a disdainful look. "I'm a traitor! You should be plotting and scheming how to bring me down, not blubbering like a sodding baby!" His eyes narrowed. "Or maybe that's what you *are* doing, eh? A feminine trick to gain my sympathy?"

"Right," she retorted softly, gingerly touching her thigh. "Because that strategy worked so well last time."

His lip twitched in a sneer, but thankfully he didn't reach for the switchblade again. "How a chit like you managed to bring us all down—me, Camara, Memebe, the whole damn European diamond trade—I'll never understand. Obviously a colossal fluke."

"Obviously." She bit back the sarcasm.

The guy was a jerk, but his words pricked at her pride. She really had been trying to come up with a plan to free herself, but the pickings were slim. He'd cuffed her wrists in front, trapping the shoulder harness part of the seat belt between her arms. So even if she'd had an opportunity to run—which she hadn't—she'd have had to cut either the cable cuffs or the seat belt before being able to escape. There was no way to pull free. The cuffs were police issue, indestructible. And seat belts were made to withstand incredible strain without giving way. An elephant couldn't have gotten loose from this car. Simple. Effective. Frustrating as hell.

But she better come up with something quick because the bumpy track they were driving along crested the top of a rocky rise, and they were greeted by the vast, churning expanse of the sea. She had a very bad feeling.

"Frightened?" Milleflora asked.

"I'd be an idiot if I weren't," she admitted, eyeing the roiling water shakily. "What are you going to do with me?" Drowning wasn't exactly her death of choice. In fact, the thought terrified her.

She'd much rather go out in a blaze of gunfire. Okay, she'd rather not go out at all.

"I've been trying to decide," he said, tilting his head thoughtfully. "On the one hand, you have behaved yourself fairly well. Didn't overly provoke me, for which I'm grateful. Yes, you are the catalyst to my present predicament, but in all fairness it was bound to happen sooner or later. It would be wrong to fault you for my lifestyle. And finally, as an agent you were really just doing your job." The last was laced with irony.

She bit her tongue. "I appreciate your objectivity."

"On the other hand," he continued as though she hadn't spoken, "you are working with Corbett Lazlo."

Her attention darted to him. "What does he have to do with anything?" She prompted.

"Lazlo used to be with MI6, you know."

"Yeah, so?"

"So, let's just say some of my best friends are his worst enemies."

She straightened, thinking immediately of Corbett—and Witt. "The Lazlo Group vendetta. It has something to do with SIS?"

His brows lifted. "I am impressed."

"You're part of it, aren't you," she said.

He laughed softly. "Me? God, no. I don't care much one way or another what happens to Lazlo. He's never hurt me personally, nor interfered in my business." Meaning Corbett *had* done so with those plotting against him? "Though I'll admit I did pass along the fact that you were meeting with him."

Another puzzle solved. "To who?" she asked.

He laughed again. "I'd tell you, but then I really would have to kill you."

"Okay, never mind." Survive first, then worry about Corbett. *Like the madman would really let her live.*

Milleflora looked away as they drove nearer the edge of the cliffs, gazing out over the roiling, crashing waves and the deep black water beyond. She held her breath, feeling the weight of his decision in the air. He wasn't that old, maybe around sixty, but as Indiana Jones once said, it wasn't the years that counted, it was the mileage. Roland Milleflora had a lot of mileage on him. She could almost feel the toll those miles had taken, in the way he seemed to look through the impenetrably dark water to something invisible, something beyond. Fate? A reckoning with God? The lost innocence of youth? She should be so lucky.

She shivered, wanting to say something. To tell him it was all right, to just take his off-shore millions and disappear. Find some island somewhere and learn to paint, or write a book. He'd served his country well for over forty years, doing things that no one else had had the stomach to do. Things that would give any normal person nightmares. Ugly things, but necessary things.

"Then why?" she asked. "Why did you do it?"

"For the money." He glanced briefly at her, then back to the sea. "And myriad other reasons, none of which a child such as you would understand."

Then again… He was a bad guy. A very bad guy.

He'd made his money from blood diamonds, one of the most despicable trades in the history of the world. He'd profited from the misery of countless souls and sent even more to their graves in unnecessary wars and outright acts of terrorism. How could she in any way absolve this man of his crimes?

"Ah," he said, and she realized he was looking at her again. There was a pained, amused look in his eyes. "Perhaps you grasp my dilemma, after all."

"No dilemma," she said. "Let me go. You can still get away. Kill me and you'll ensure the Lazlo Group, at the very least, will hunt you down no matter what cave you crawl into."

He pursed his lips. "Your boyfriend, I presume. The one whose life you saved by killing Camara."

She nodded. As DDG of SIS, Milleflora knew exactly what had gone down at the warehouse that morning. He knew all about her, so she wasn't surprised he knew about Witt, too. "Agent von Kreus is a pretty single-minded guy. And Corbett Lazlo is a family friend. He'll take it as a personal affront if you kill me."

"I'm beginning to understand why my friends consider him such a nuisance."

She tried again. In case she somehow made it out of this alive. "Enough of a nuisance to want him dead?"

"Not just dead," Milleflora corrected. "Humiliated. Ruined. Broken. Only then will he be given the mercy of death. And Camara's elimination is a blow they won't forget."

"But Corbett had nothing to do with that."

"On the contrary. He was running the whole operation this morning. The blood diamonds were an important source of their funding."

"Who *are* these people?"

"Enough of this," Milleflora said as he drove the car right up to the very edge of the cliff. "Lazlo is not my concern. You, however, are."

The clouds parted to reveal a chunk of moon, which reflected glittering yellow off the water as the turbulent waves crashed into the steep, rocky cliffs below. It was like a scene out of a Daphne du Maurier novel. Bleak. Sinister. Treacherous.

Marina glanced at him. He smiled back. It was not a nice smile.

A sudden, choking terror swept through her.

Oh, God. *This was it.*

Chapter 13

Witt had never jumped out of a helicopter before, but he wasn't about to stay behind because of that. Nor was he going to let a mere gunshot wound stop him, either. They'd pinpointed Marina's minitracker to a remote section of seacoast in Pembroke County in the south of Wales, and Witt planned to be on the front line when the military assault team landed to intercept…even if it was dark as pitch out, with only the dimmest part of a waning moon to light their way.

Their orders were clear. Capture Milleflora any way they had to, dead or alive. Witt did not like Marina's chances if the bullets started flying. Assuming she was still alive. The tracking beacon hadn't moved for over fifteen minutes. Not a good sign. Either she was immobilized or the tracker had gotten wet and shorted out.

He was battling to stay calm. Panic would do no one any good. But it was tough, especially when all he wanted was to wrap his hands around someone's neck. Preferably Milleflora.

The first helo dropped a team of divers into the black water with their MAV—motorized amphibious vehicle—several hundred meters out from shore. Witt was in the second helo with one of the two land teams. He held his bad arm close to his chest and jumped from the bay when he was told to jump, landing hard on the rocky ground at the top of the cliffs in the orange circle of a spotlight that was aimed down from the copter. He rolled onto all threes, tested his legs and arm and found they all worked. More or less. Amazing what adrenaline and painkillers could do for a body. One-handed, he swung his machine gun forward from where it was strapped on his back and started crouch-running with the other three guys toward the tracker signal's last coordinates, on the other side of a giant craggy rock. Each man was armed with multiple weapons, high-tech night-vision goggles and a helmet-mounted LED light, which if switched on would light up the darkness in conical slices of brightness.

When they rounded the crag, everyone stopped short. There was no car in sight. No Milleflora.

And no Marina.

A shout came from the second land team, which

had jumped from a third helo and was now approaching from the other direction. Their LED lights were all pointing down at the bottom of the cliffs.

Witt cursed and started to sprint. He barely stopped himself when he got to the edge. What he saw made him want to hurl himself over the cliff.

A car had crash-landed nose first on the jagged rocks below and was engulfed in flames. There was no sign of life anywhere.

The ten grueling minutes it took Witt to rappel one-armed down the face of the cliff to the wrecked vehicle with the rest of the team were the longest minutes of his life. The other land team had fanned out to search above, in case the car was just a diversion. He prayed it was. If Marina was injured or dead…

No. He wouldn't go there. If he started thinking about it, he'd lose his mind.

By the time they reached the car, the fire had nearly burned itself out. The heat radiating from the charred metal skeleton was blistering hot, but Witt shielded his face and got as close as he could. He had to know if Marina was inside.

She couldn't be. She just couldn't be.

Pulse pounding like a sharp mallet against the back of his throat, he peered in through the broken-out passenger-side window.

For an endless moment his heart stopped, then leaped to life again.

She wasn't there!

Nobody was.

"They're not in the car!" he shouted, spinning to examine the cliff face, sweeping his LED light over the vertical rock for possible hiding places. He picked out a path leading to what looked like a yawning sea cave. "There!"

The team rushed into the cave, weapons at the ready. Not a glint of moonlight found its way past the low-ceilinged entrance. Even the team's high-intensity helmet lights barely dimmed the darkness. Someone switched on a powerful spot flashlight, followed by another.

Witt squinted against the sudden brightness and glanced around. The entrance of the huge main room had ample water access from the sea, but the back of the cavern was high and dry, except for a narrow channel of water that led deeper into the bowels of the earth. A small side crevice provided the obligatory escape route. It was now blocked by Witt and the others.

The place was like something you'd read about in an old pirate novel. The perfect spot for a bit of smuggling. Milleflora must have kept a getaway boat here in case he needed a quick exit from the country.

Inside, the team halted on a shallow ledge and stayed perfectly still, listening carefully for any movement above the echoing ebb and flow of the water just below.

All at once he heard it. A muffled cry.

A *woman's* muffled cry.

"Marina!" Witt shouted, breaking the tense silence. "Marina! Where are you?"

Suddenly the sound of an engine roared to life and blasted through the cavern. Flashlight beams swung wildly, converging on the source. A rubber dinghy burst from the darkness of the narrow back channel, running full speed ahead in a zig-zag pattern toward the sea entrance.

Milleflora was hunched at the rear holding a large automatic pistol in one hand, steering with the other like a madman. Marina knelt in front, gagged, her arms bound behind her and clinging desperately to the side with her fingers so she wouldn't be thrown out of the boat. Witt could see her ankles were bound together, too. As the dinghy sped past the ledge, she turned her head and blinked owl-like into the focused flashlight beams.

She was looking for Witt. He could feel it.

Milleflora suddenly swung his gun around and pointed at them. Directly at Witt. Marina's eyes widened above her gag and he heard another muffled cry. Suddenly she hurled herself at Milleflora, knocking them both from the boat just as his first shot went off.

Herre Yessus! She was bound and gagged.

Witt didn't even think. He just dove into the frigid water after her. If he didn't reach her she'd drown.

Milleflora surfaced quickly and his curses filled the air. He shot wild, the sound ricocheting around the cave walls like thunder. Marina's head bobbed up for a brief moment, then went under again. Milleflora swam a beeline toward her, aiming his gun at the spot she'd disappeared. A volley of shots blasted from behind Witt, and the water around Milleflora bloomed red. Witt threw off his sling and swam like a madman, diving and groping the water desperately to find Marina.

There! He felt the long strands of her hair.

He dove again and suddenly she was in his arms and he was pulling her up from the freezing water. He ripped Marina's gag off so she could breathe better. She took a big gulp of air. He lifted her high in his good arm and swam toward land as best he could.

The assault team had plunged in after Milleflora, joined by the divers that sped into the cavern on the MAV. Splashing and yelling, both teams swarmed over the wounded fugitive, making a clean capture.

Witt dragged Marina up onto dry land and sat her on the sand, moving his good hand over her in the darkness to check for wounds and anything that might be broken. His other hand had lost feeling.

"Marina! Marina are you all right, *skat?*" he demanded, kneeling in front of her. "Talk to me, *liefde.*"

"Th-the handcuffs," she said through chattering teeth. As soon as he cut the cable cuffs binding her, she threw her arms around him. "I'm fine." But she clung to him as if she never wanted to let go. "The bastard was going to drown me!"

Witt kissed her cheeks and forehead and eyes, sending up a silent prayer of thanks for her safety. He held her close and rocked her against his chest. "You didn't really think I'd let him, did you?"

For a moment the darkness pressed in around

them, thick and blanketing. "No. I knew you'd come." Even her shivers had trembles as she said on a hitched breath, "You never did trust me to take care of myself." But she only clung harder and added, "Thank God."

He smiled in relief and hugged her again fiercely. "I take it that's not a complaint this time."

"I swear I'll never complain again about you wanting to take care of me. Not ever."

At the choked-out words, his hopes soared. Not daring to believe what he thought he was hearing, he released her enough to peer into her eyes. "Really?"

She shook her head. "Never, ever," she whispered, her voice cracking. A flashlight caught them it its bright beam, and she quickly looked away. But not before he saw the glint of tears in her eyes.

He was hit with a surge of emotion so swift and hard his breath caught painfully in his lungs.

"Marina," he whispered, tilting her face up to him with his fingers. He tenderly wiped the moisture away with his thumbs. "If you truly mean that, let me take care of you for real. For always."

Rivulets of water from her wet hair dripped onto her face and trailed down her forehead and cheeks as she stared at him uncomprehendingly. Even drenched like a drowned rat and blue-lipped from the cold, she was the most beautiful woman in the world. He loved her so much his heart ached with it.

"What are you saying, Witt?" The tentative words were so softly spoken he could barely hear them.

Had he done that to her? Made her so uncertain

of their future, so unsure of his feelings for her that she questioned them like this? A lump formed in his throat. Looked like old Sam Barlow was right. Time to set things straight. And time to let go of the past.

"I'm saying I want you with me, *skat*. I want you to move to Paris and be with me. I—" he swallowed heavily "—I love you, Marina. Please, for pity's sake, put me out of my misery and marry me."

Her mouth dropped open and for several seconds her teeth stopped chattering as she gazed at him in astonishment.

All at once he was scared to death. Maybe he'd misinterpreted their relationship, her feelings. Maybe she really *didn't* want him. Maybe that's why she ran away to London without a word. Because she didn't love him, and had taken him at his word that he was only interested in sex, not a long-term commitment. Because that's what she wanted, too.

"Okay," she said.

He blinked in confusion. And tried to think. "Okay?"

Her teeth started chattering again. "Okay, I'll marry you."

This time *his* mouth dropped open. For about a nanosecond. Then a huge smile broke through his whole being and he pulled her close and kissed her over and over.

"On one condition," she added, laughing and shivering as she returned his kisses.

"Anything," he assured her, knowing he would go

anywhere, do anything, to be with this amazing woman for the rest of his life.

"I want a roaring fire, a hot toddy and to get out of these wet clothes," she said, eyes sparkling like emeralds.

"I believe," he said, heart soaring as he pulled her closer into his arms, "that can be arranged."

The fire was wonderful, Marina thought with a contented sigh.

The toddy—mulled wine, actually—was wonderful.

Witt was wonderful. Even if he was passed out.

Poor guy. This was the second time he'd ripped out the stitches in his shoulder. Jumping out of a helicopter and rappelling down a cliff had probably not been the greatest idea. The local Welsh doctor that was summoned last night had just shaken his head, restitched the gaping wound and given Witt a shot in the backside that had knocked him out almost instantly.

"Make him stay in the room for four days," the doctor had told her sternly before leaving the cozy suite in the charming bed-and-breakfast they'd checked into after their harrowing ordeal in the cave. "Preferably in bed."

Marina had nodded somberly, assuring the doctor she would make sure Witt didn't stray from the bed or the giant clawfoot tub in the en suite master bath.

Oh, yes. Life was very good.

She was now curled up next to him on the huge, canopied antique four-poster, a fire burning contentedly in the grate, lacy window curtains drawn on a sparkling blue sea and a delicious luncheon wafting mouthwatering aromas from a silver tray on the bedside table.

"Mmm," he hummed without opening his eyes. How long had he been awake? "I must have died from my wounds. For surely I'm in heaven."

She grinned and kissed him on the cheek. "That's right. And you're stuck here on this cloud with me for all eternity."

He hummed again, his smile widening. "Beauty." He shifted his good arm, putting it around her, scooting her closer to him as he opened his eyes to look at her. "What *will* we do for all that time?"

"Oh...I'm pretty sure we can think of something."

"But you don't play the harp. And I've heard you sing....."

"Oh!" she cried in mock indignation, sitting up to swat him in the arm—the good one.

"Hey! Wounded man!" he protested, sweeping her back into his embrace. He pulled her down onto his chest. "Wounded man who's finally found the permanent cure for his pain."

She smiled up at him. "I'll take good care of you, Witt, I promise. When I move in—"

"Wait a minute," he cut her off with a finger to her lips. "I know I asked you to quit SIS and move to Paris, but I realize I was being selfish. Now that Milleflora is behind bars and Jenkins is spilling his guts, there's no danger. I can move to London. Corbett won't mind."

She gazed at him in disbelief, her soul filling with warmth. "You'd do that? For me?"

"God, yes. I'd go anywhere to be with you, *liefde.*"

"You would?"

"Absolutely anywhere."

She hugged him close, shaking her head. "Not necessary. I phoned in my resignation to Dalgliesh this morning."

"But you love your job at SIS," Witt objected. "And you're great at it."

His praise put a lump in her throat. It was as though an inner tension she hadn't known was there suddenly relaxed and uncoiled. "It means the world to me to hear you say that. But I'll love my new job just, as well."

He looked uncertain. "New job?"

She took a deep breath, hoping what she was about to say pleased him. "At the Lazlo Group. I asked Corbett about the possibility last night when we talked on the phone."

Witt's face clouded over. "You did *what? Yerre, skat!* The Lazlo Group is the last place I want you working! Someone out there is killing Lazlo agents. Until we catch them—"

"I want to help put these people away. Witt, I owe Corbett my life. And now I owe you, too."

He shook his head. "The only thing either of us wants is for you to be safe."

"I know." She kissed him, needing him to see how important this decision was to her. "And I appreciate that. But this way we can all keep each other safe."

He let out a long breath. "I'm not going to be able to change your mind about this, am I?"

She shook her head with a wistful smile. "I'd hoped you'd be happy we'll be together."

"Oh, *skat*." He folded her back in his arm. "I am. Truly I am. Just give me a little time to get used to the idea."

She nestled down against him. "That's okay. We have all the time in the world. A lifetime."

"A lifetime…" He broke into a smile and kissed her, then gazed down at her tenderly, hesitantly. "Marina I still can't believe… Did you really say yes? I didn't dream or hallucinate it? You really said you'd marry me?"

Her heart squeezed at the almost terrified hope in his eyes. "No, it wasn't a dream. Yes, I really said I'd marry you," she assured him and hugged him closer.

"Are you…are you sure?" he asked softly, and her heart almost broke.

"I've never been as sure of anything in my life," she whispered.

"But a man like me, how can you—"

"A man like you? You mean a good man? A man who's loyal and honorable and strong, and so incredibly sexy he takes my breath away?"

His eyes grew suddenly shiny and his Adam's apple bobbed up and down. "Not exactly what I was thinking, but it'll do," he said, his voice rough with emotion.

Her breath hitched in her lungs, her whole being bursting with love for this tortured hero, this perfect man. "I love you, Witt. I never knew it was possible to love a person as much as I love you. I want to be with you forever."

She felt a tremor go through his body as his arm banded her against him fiercely and held her so close she thought their bodies might meld together as one.

"I love you, too, Marina," he whispered. "You'll never know how very much I love you. Have loved you since the first moment I saw you."

She choked out a watery laugh, so overflowing with love she felt she would float away from pure happiness. "Must have been the Denmark protocol."

He laughed, too, the sound filled with joy and love and tenderness and desire, his eyes brimming with the promise of a bright, shining future. "No, *liefde*. It was you. And it will always be you."

She touched his cheek and kissed his lips and knew at last he was hers, her man for forever.

"Us," she whispered. "It will always be us, together."

* * * * *

Don't miss the next exciting
MISSION: IMPASSIONED *novel!*
BULLETPROOF MARRIAGE by Karen Whiddon
available October 2007, only from
Silhouette Romantic Suspense.

For a sneak preview of Marie Ferrarella's
DOCTOR IN THE HOUSE,
coming to NEXT in September,
please turn the page.

He didn't look like an unholy terror.

But maybe that reputation was exaggerated, Bailey Del Monico thought as she turned in her chair to look toward the doorway.

The man didn't seem scary at all.

Dr. Munro, or Ivan the Terrible, was tall, with an athletic build and wide shoulders. The cheekbones beneath what she estimated to be day-old stubble were prominent. His hair was light brown and just this side of unruly. Munro's hair looked as if he used his fingers for a comb and didn't care who knew it.

The eyes were brown, almost black as they were aimed at her. There was no other word for it. Aimed. As if he was debating whether or not to fire at point-blank range.

Somewhere in the back of her mind, a line from a B movie, "Be afraid—be very afraid…" whispered along the perimeter of her brain. Warning her. Almost against her will, it caused her to brace her shoulders. Bailey had to remind herself to breathe in and out like a normal person.

The chief of staff, Dr. Bennett, had tried his level

best to put her at ease and had almost succeeded. But an air of tension had entered with Munro. She wondered if Dr. Bennett was bracing himself as well, bracing for some kind of disaster or explosion.

"Ah, here he is now," Harold Bennett announced needlessly. The smile on his lips was slightly forced, and the look in his gray, kindly eyes held a warning as he looked at his chief neurosurgeon. "We were just talking about you, Dr. Munro."

"Can't imagine why," Ivan replied dryly.

Harold cleared his throat, as if that would cover the less than friendly tone of voice Ivan had just displayed. "Dr. Munro, this is the young woman I was telling you about yesterday."

Now his eyes dissected her. Bailey felt as if she was undergoing a scalpel-less autopsy right then and there. "Ah yes, the Stanford Special."

He made her sound like something that was listed at the top of a third-rate diner menu. There was enough contempt in his voice to offend an entire delegation from the UN.

Summoning the bravado that her parents always claimed had been infused in her since the moment she first drew breath, Bailey put out her hand. "Hello. I'm Dr. Bailey DelMonico."

Ivan made no effort to take the hand offered to him. Instead, he slid his long, lanky form bonelessly into the chair beside her. He proceeded to move the chair ever so slightly so that there was even more space between them. Ivan faced the chief of staff, but the words he spoke were addressed to her.

"You're a doctor, Del Monico, when I say you're a doctor," he informed her coldly, sparing her only one frosty glance to punctuate the end of his statement.

Harold stifled a sigh. "Dr. Munro is going to take over your education. Dr. Munro—" he fixed Ivan with a steely gaze that had been known to send lesser doctors running for their antacids, but, as always, seemed to have no effect on the chief neurosurgeon "—I want you to award her every consideration. From now on, Dr. DelMonico is to be your shadow, your sponge and your assistant." He emphasized the last word as his eyes locked with Ivan's. "Do I make myself clear?"

For his part, Ivan seemed completely unfazed. He merely nodded, his eyes and expression unreadable. "Perfectly."

His hand was on the doorknob. Bailey sprang to her feet. Her chair made a scraping noise as she moved it back and then quickly joined the neurosurgeon before he could leave the office.

Closing the door behind him, Ivan leaned over and whispered into her ear, "Just so you know, I'm going to be your worst nightmare."

Bailey DelMonico has finally
gotten her life on track, and is
passionate about her recent career
change. Nothing will stand in the way
of her becoming a doctor...that is,
until she's paired with the sharp-tongued
Dr. Ivan Munro.

Watch the sparks fly in

Doctor in
the House

by *USA TODAY* Bestselling Author

Marie Ferrarella

Available September 2007

Intrigued? Read more at
TheNextNovel.com

HARLEQUIN®

Mediterranean NIGHTS™

Sail aboard the luxurious Alexandra's Dream and experience glamour, romance, mystery and revenge!

Coming in October 2007...

AN AFFAIR TO REMEMBER

by

Karen Kendall

When Captain Nikolas Pappas first fell in love with Helena Stamos, he was a penniless deckhand and she was the daughter of a shipping magnate. But he's never forgiven himself for the way he left her—and fifteen years later, he's determined to win her back.

Though the attraction is still there, Helena is hesitant to get involved. Nick left her once...what's to stop him from doing it again?

HM38964

REQUEST YOUR FREE BOOKS!

2 FREE NOVELS PLUS 2 FREE GIFTS!

Silhouette® Romantic

SUSPENSE

Sparked by Danger, Fueled by Passion!

YES! Please send me 2 FREE Silhouette® Romantic Suspense novels and my 2 FREE gifts. After receiving them, if I don't wish to receive any more books, I can return the shipping statement marked "cancel." If I don't cancel, I will receive 4 brand-new novels every month and be billed just $4.24 per book in the U.S., or $4.99 per book in Canada, plus 25¢ shipping and handling per book plus applicable taxes, if any*. That's a savings of at least 15% off the cover price! I understand that accepting the 2 free books and gifts places me under no obligation to buy anything. I can always return a shipment and cancel at any time. Even if I never buy another book from Silhouette, the two free books and gifts are mine to keep forever.

240 SDN EEX6 340 SDN EEYJ

Name	(PLEASE PRINT)

Address	Apt. #

City	State/Prov.	Zip/Postal Code

Signature (if under 18, a parent or guardian must sign)

Mail to the Silhouette Reader Service™:
IN U.S.A.: P.O. Box 1867, Buffalo, NY 14240-1867
IN CANADA: P.O. Box 609, Fort Erie, Ontario L2A 5X3

Not valid to current Silhouette Intimate Moments subscribers.

Want to try two free books from another line?
Call 1-800-873-8635 or visit www.morefreebooks.com.

* Terms and prices subject to change without notice. NY residents add applicable sales tax. Canadian residents will be charged applicable provincial taxes and GST. This offer is limited to one order per household. All orders subject to approval. Credit or debit balances in a customer's account(s) may be offset by any other outstanding balance owed by or to the customer. Please allow 4 to 6 weeks for delivery.

Your Privacy: Silhouette is committed to protecting your privacy. Our Privacy Policy is available online at www.eHarlequin.com or upon request from the Reader Service. From time to time we make our lists of customers available to reputable firms who may have a product or service of interest to you. If you would prefer we not share your name and address, please check here. ☐

SRS07

The latest novel in The Lakeshore Chronicles
by *New York Times* bestselling author

SUSAN WIGGS

From the award-winning author of *Summer at Willow Lake*
comes an unforgettable story of a woman's emotional journey
from the heartache of the past to hope for the future.

With her daughter grown and flown, Nina Romano is ready to
embark on a new adventure. She's waited a long time for dating,
travel and chasing dreams. But just as she's beginning to enjoy
being on her own, she finds herself falling for Greg Bellamy,
owner of the charming Inn at Willow Lake and a single father
with two kids of his own.

DOCKSIDE

"The perfect summer read." —Debbie Macomber

*Available the first week of August 2007
wherever paperbacks are sold!*

Silhouette Desire

There was only one man for the job—
an impossible-to-resist maverick
she knew she didn't dare fall for.

MAVERICK
(#1827)

BY *NEW YORK TIMES*
BESTSELLING AUTHOR
JOAN HOHL

"Will You Do It for One Million Dollars?"

Any other time, Tanner Wolfe would have balked at being
hired by a woman. Yet Brianna Stewart was desperate to
engage the infamous bounty hunter. The price was just
high enough to gain Tanner's interest…Brianna's beauty
definitely strong enough to keep it. But he wasn't about
to allow her to tag along on his mission. He worked
alone. Always had. Always would. However, he'd never
confronted a more determined client than Brianna. She
wasn't taking no for an answer—not about anything.

Perhaps a million-dollar bounty was not the only thing
this maverick was about to gain….

Look for MAVERICK

Available October 2007 wherever you buy books.

Silhouette®
Romantic
SUSPENSE

Sparked by Danger, Fueled by Passion.

When evidence is found that Mallory Dawes intends to sell the personal financial information of government employees to "the Russian," OMEGA engages undercover agent Cutter Smith. Tailing her all the way to France, Cutter is fighting a growing attraction to Mallory while at the same time having to determine her connection to "the Russian." Is Mallory really the mouse in this game of cat and mouse?

Look for

Stranded with a Spy

by *USA TODAY* bestselling author

Merline Lovelace

October 2007.

Also available October wherever you buy books:
BULLETPROOF MARRIAGE *(Mission: Impassioned)*
by Karen Whiddon
A HERO'S REDEMPTION *(Haven)* by Suzanne McMinn
TOUCHED BY FIRE by Elizabeth Sinclair

Romantic

SUSPENSE

COMING NEXT MONTH

#1483 STRANDED WITH A SPY—Merline Lovelace
Code Name: Danger
When evidence suggests that Mallory Dawes intends to sell government information, OMEGA undercover agent Cutter Smith is sent to investigate. But a complex game of cat and mouse ensues as he fights his growing attraction for Mallory.

#1484 BULLETPROOF MARRIAGE—Karen Whiddon
Mission: Impassioned
Secret agent Sean McGregor fakes his own death when a madman murdered his family and targeted his wife. Now he must return from the shadows to save the woman with whom he once shared his life.

#1485 A HERO'S REDEMPTION—Suzanne McMinn
Haven
Caught in a supernatural time shift, Dane McGuire is taken back to the week of Calla Jone's death—and he'll be convicted of murder if he can't stop the past. But along the way he develops an intense desire for the woman he may ultimately kill.

#1486 TOUCHED BY FIRE—Elizabeth Sinclair
The last person firefighter Samantha Ellis wants protecting her is Detective AJ Branson. The arrogant, sexy detective spells trouble, but with a maniac out to kill her, AJ seems to be the only one who can save her—and steal her heart.